730L/8 •

MW00769004

deleted

12-8-17

UNCLE DANEY'S WAY

by Jessie Haas

A BEECH TREE PAPERBACK BOOK   NEW YORK

Thanks to Jay Bailey, Wayne Bartlett,
and Sonny Brown, who show us how
every year at the Deerfield Valley Fair

The Library of Congress has cataloged
the Greenwillow Books edition of
Uncle Daney's Way as follows:
Haas, Jessie.
Uncle Daney's way / by Jessie Haas.
p. cm.
Summary: When his great-uncle Daney comes to live with Cole's
family after being crippled in a logging accident, the two work
together all summer to find a way to make enough money to buy
feed so they can keep Daney's old horse.
ISBN 0-688-12794-0
[1. Great-uncles—Fiction. 2. Horses—Fiction. 3. Country
life—Fiction.] I. Title.
PZ7.H1129Un 1994 [Fic]—dc20
93-22192 CIP AC

1 3 5 7 9 10 8 6 4 2
First Beech Tree Edition, 1997
ISBN 0-688-15491-3

TO MOM,
FOR OBVIOUS REASONS

Uncle Daney's Way

|| CHAPTER ONE ||

WHEN UNCLE DANEY got out of the hospital, there was no place to put him but the barn.

"I think it's terrible!" Mom said. She and Pop had just gotten home from visiting Uncle Daney.

But Pop said, "Lou, that barn is a palace, compared with the places he's been living. Heck, it's a palace compared with this trailer!"

"Why does he have to live with us, anyway?" Cole asked. He knew that Uncle Daney was a logger and that he had been in an accident back in the winter. But when Mom and Pop left this morning, there had been no talk of this.

"They say his legs won't get any better. He has to be in a wheelchair, and he doesn't have anybody else."

"And you can see what it would be like, having a

wheelchair in here." Pop looked the length of the trailer. From where he sat at the table he could see most of it, narrow and crowded, and all in a straight line.

"We could *manage*," Mom said, but Cole didn't think so. Even when it was just the three of them, all with good legs, they bumped into one another too often. Cole had always lived in trailers, but the one they'd had back in the trailer park had been big and new.

"The barn's easy to get in and out of," Pop said. "I won't have to build a ramp. And we won't be on top of each other every minute of the day. It was his own idea, Lou. I don't see how we can tell him no."

Mom snorted. "Nobody can ever tell Uncle Daney no!"

After supper Pop and Cole put on their jackets and went out to the barn. The air felt soft and warm on their faces. It smelled like mud, like spring.

When Pop snapped on the lights, the barn became a huge yellow cave. The beams cast dark bars of shadow across the wide central aisle. On each side of the aisle were three stall doors, bottoms closed, tops open and dark. On top of each bank of stalls was the platform for storing hay. The platforms were dark and shadowy, too, and empty.

Pop pushed the big door farther back on its roller and bent down to look where the driveway met the threshold. "Smooth enough," he said. "He'll be able to get in and out, no problem."

Now Pop pulled open the door of the first stall.

It was like a little room, with tightly fitting board walls all the way up to the ceiling and a tight board floor, roughened by horses' hooves. This was a rich person's horse barn. Once there had been a rich person's house where the trailer now stood. It had burned down a few years ago, and that was why Mom and Pop could afford to buy this place. Just barely afford it.

"You'll have to move all this stuff out," Pop said. Cole had used the stall to store sap buckets and the boiling pans when he had finished sugaring a couple of weeks ago.

"Okay."

"I guess we'll have to sand this floor, too. That won't be good for a wheelchair."

"There's a bump here at the threshold," Cole said.

"We can build a wedge in there."

Cole shoved his hands deep in his jacket pockets, frowning at the stall. This was going to be a lot of work, and that was good. Now that sugaring season was through, he didn't have much to do after school.

But it wasn't fair. *He* wanted to live out here. From the first day they'd moved here, almost a year ago, he'd been planning how to make one of these stalls into a room for himself. He'd even asked once or twice. Mom and Pop might not be able to say no to Uncle Daney, but they could say no to *him*, loud and clear!

And anyway, why couldn't they say no to Uncle Daney? Loggers drank a lot, Cole knew. They were rough on their horses, and if they had families, they were rough on them, too. Pop seemed to think this barn was a palace, and maybe he'd described it that way to Uncle Daney. But what if Uncle Daney didn't agree?

"You think it'll be okay?" he asked.

"Oh, yeah," Pop said. "It's nice and tight. Good big window—"

"No. I mean, will he like it?"

"We'll start work on it tomorrow," Pop said. He didn't sound worried, so Cole kept his doubts to himself.

They had a week to get ready. For Cole it was a good week, in spite of everything. In the afternoons, when the empty school bus turned around in his driveway and let him off, he had work to do. He didn't have to invent something. He didn't have to walk alone up the Hogback, the huge dark hill that rose behind the trailer, blocking out the sun. He didn't have to wish for some wood to stack or even for more homework.

Monday he moved the sap buckets and swept down the cobwebs from the ceiling. He ripped the wooden bars off the window with a crowbar, and he washed the window inside and out. There was an iron hayrack in one corner, and he left that. It would make a good place to store things.

That night Pop brought home lumber and helped Cole

draw up plans to make the half door into a solid door. Over the next few days Cole rebuilt the door himself.

He liked having it to think about at school. Even though he'd been in this school for all of seventh grade now, he didn't fit in. His clothes were different. He wore homemade shirts and work boots instead of running shoes. His hair was cut just like Pop's. Only Roger Allard looked and dressed the way Cole did, but Roger fitted in fine. He didn't seem to need another friend. So Cole was glad to have the plans for Uncle Daney's door to tinker with in his free time. At least it made him look as if he was too busy to care.

Pop borrowed a sander and smoothed the floor out. He got Uncle Daney a heater, and he put in plumbing. Pop could do most of the work himself, but still, the lumber and supplies cost more than he could really afford.

Mom swept, vacuumed, washed, and aired the stall. On Friday afternoon, when it was clean and fresh-smelling, she and Cole brought in the table and the chest of drawers they'd gotten from the secondhand store, and set up the iron bed frame. When it was together, Mom stood back with her hands on her hips and looked around the stall.

"It's not that bad," she said. "If I put some curtains in the window and get him a rug—"

"A carpet would be better," Cole said. "For the wheelchair."

"You're right," said Mom. "And if I know Uncle Daney, he won't be interested in how it looks, anyway!" She took the sheets out of her basket to make up the bed.

"Do you *like* him?" Cole asked.

Mom's hands slowed in surprise. Cole couldn't see her face. "Yes," she said after a moment. "Everybody likes Uncle Daney."

The next day was Saturday, and a friend of Uncle Daney's was going to bring him down from the hospital. Mom got Pop and Cole up early because nobody knew when Uncle Daney would arrive. But he didn't come at breakfast, and he didn't come while Pop sat at the table and slowly finished his second cup of coffee.

"Well, I can't just sit," Pop said. "Might as well cut some wood."

He and Cole went out to the pasture. It flowed like a river along the bottom of the Hogback, choked with big juniper bushes and wild roses. There was barely enough grass for the one steer Pop was raising.

Where the pasture fence came close behind the trailer was the pile of logs Pop had dragged down from the Hogback last fall. Pop cut trees all year round, but he could get the logs down only at the end of corn-chopping season, when he could borrow somebody's tractor.

Pop ran the chain saw. Cole helped him move and balance the logs and rolled the chunks of firewood out of his way. The chain saw made a horrible noise, and

Cole was glad he was too young to run it. When he was a few years older, he would have to run a chain saw. When Cole was old enough, and when Pop had saved enough money to buy his own tractor, they were going to go into business selling firewood. Then Pop wouldn't have to work at the paper mill anymore.

Pop shouldn't have to work in a paper mill, Cole thought. That was why they'd moved out here, where they could grow their own food and cut their own wood, make a little maple syrup, and maybe get ahead. But Cole still wished that somebody, soon, would invent a quiet chain saw.

While they worked, Cole kept his eye on the road. He felt strange working out here like any normal Saturday when any minute now everything was going to change. Uncle Daney was coming to live with them. He wasn't going away. Somebody Cole had never met—and a logger, a kind of person he'd heard only bad things about. A logger in a wheelchair. All week, while Pop was at work and Cole at school, Mom would be home alone with him. Cole's stomach began to feel as if he had broken bottles in the bottom of it, shifting and scraping around.

Finally, late in the morning, he saw a big green livestock truck slow down and disappear behind the trailer. After a minute Mom came to the corner and waved.

Cole touched Pop on the shoulder. He turned off the chain saw, and they walked around to the front.

The truck was parked there, next to the barn, and as

Pop and Cole came around the corner, the driver's door opened.

The man who got out was huge and bald, with silver fur on his face. It wan't curly like a beard, and it wasn't long enough. It looked about the length of cat's fur.

The man nodded hello and let down the ramp of his truck. Now Cole heard a heavy thump and scrape inside. Must be a horse in there, he thought.

The man ran up the ramp, quicker than a man that size usually moves, and came back down wheeling a wheelchair. In the chair was a worn old suitcase, and slung over the man's shoulder was a bulging denim laundry bag. He put the bag and suitcase on the ground and wheeled the chair up beside the passenger door. Cole could see somebody in the cab, but he couldn't see much of him. He seemed to be slumped way down in the seat. Cole wondered just how sick Uncle Daney was.

"I'll give you a hand," Pop said, stepping forward. But the silver-furred man already had the door open. He reached inside, and when he turned around, he held a little old man in his arms.

It must be a mistake! thought Cole. They switched them in the hospital!

The big man settled the little man gently into the wheelchair and turned him around to face them.

"Oh, Uncle Daney!" Mom said, laughing. "Did you lose your teeth?"

The old man's sunken mouth widened in a pink cackle. "Heh-heh-heh! Them nurses made me wear 'em all the time!" His words were mushy and hard to understand.

"But did you *bring* them?" Mom asked, bending down to kiss his forehead, close to where his wispy white hair began. "I've got other things to do besides chew your food for you, Uncle Daney!"

"Ay-yup! Right here!" Uncle Daney fumbled in his pocket and brought out a complete set of chompers. He clacked them in his fingers, near Mom's nose, and she laughed again.

"Hello, Daney," Pop said. He reached down and shook Uncle Daney's hand. "How you doin'?"

Uncle Daney slid his teeth into his mouth and settled them into place, like a cow chewing its cud. "I'm doin' all right, Bill." With his teeth in, his voice was clearer, high and piping like a bird's. He *couldn't* be a logger, Cole thought. Maybe he was a supervisor. Maybe he'd been sitting in his office one day and a file cabinet had fallen on him—

"Who's that behind you?" Uncle Daney asked. He was craning his neck to look past Pop.

"This is our son, Cole," Pop said. He put the flat of his hand on Cole's back and swept him forward.

Cole reached down, and Uncle Daney reached up. His hand wasn't much bigger than Cole's, but his palm was hard and rough, as if it had been cut with a knife a hundred times. His face had lines running down it, like the lines spring runoff carves in hillside soil. He looked very old. But his eyes, meeting Cole's, seemed twice as alive as anybody else's, so bright and curious that Cole drew back in surprise. "Glad to meet you," Uncle Daney said. "This here's Stewie Turner." The big man behind him nodded once more.

"Well, all right, Stew," said Uncle Daney. "Let's bring him out now." The big man started to push the chair toward the back of the truck, but Uncle Daney held up his hand. "Nope, I'll push myself. You go on up in there and untie him. Speak to him gentle now."

Stewie nodded and disappeared up the ramp. Uncle Daney slowly wheeled himself toward the back of the truck. His wiry arms worked strongly, and the wheelchair tires crunched on the gravel. Mom and Pop and Cole all looked at one another. "What . . . ?" Pop said, and Mom shook her head.

They heard Stewie's voice for the first time, a low, wordless booming within the truck. Then more thuds and scrapes, the rattle of a chain . . .

"Stay back out of his way!" Uncle Daney said as Cole came close to the ramp. *Thud thud thud thud.*

Down the ramp stepped a big red workhorse, with a tousled blond mane and a sleepy face. He stopped at the bottom and stood there, looking mild and puzzled. Slowly Uncle Daney wheeled his chair closer. The horse turned his head and bent to sniff the wheels. His head alone seemed as big as Uncle Daney's whole upper body.

"Uncle Daney!" Mom said. "What—what is this?"

Uncle Daney reached for the rope, and Stewie gave it to him. Still holding the rope, he slowly turned the chair to face them. "This here's Nip," he said. "My skiddin' horse."

|| CHAPTER TWO ||

THIS WAS THE FIRST Cole had heard of Uncle Daney's bringing a horse with him. From the way Mom's and Pop's mouths hung open, it was news to them, too.

Uncle Daney looked from one to the other. His eyes, under bushy white brows, were gentle.

"Nip'll want to stretch his legs," he suggested after a moment.

Pop looked at Mom and shrugged helplessly. "Out this way, Daney. Want me to take him?"

Uncle Daney shook his head. "No, no! He'll follow me." He turned his chair. Nip raised his head slightly and looked at the shiny wheels. He seemed vaguely alarmed.

"Walk, Nip," Uncle Daney said. He draped the lead rope over his shoulder and let go of it, then used both hands to move the chair. It crunched forward, and the slack loop of rope stretched to a straight line. Just when it looked as if the rope would fall off Uncle Daney's shoulder, Nip lifted one big foot and set it down—crunch. Step by step, almost in slow motion, he followed Uncle Daney's wheelchair out behind the trailer.

Where the grass started, the chair bumped and stopped. Pop made a move to go help but stopped himself. They watched Uncle Daney maneuver, taking the smoothest path over the grass, reaching far back to get a good grip on the wheels, and hauling himself over the bumps. Nip followed, stopping whenever Uncle Daney stopped.

Pop went ahead to the barway. He drew back the bars and let them drop to the ground. Uncle Daney wheeled through the gate, with Nip behind him. When they both were inside the pasture, Uncle Daney stopped and turned.

"Head down," he said. Nip lowered his huge head till his nose rested in Uncle Daney's lap. Uncle Daney unbuckled the halter and slipped it off.

"Go on, now! Kick up your heels," he said.

Nip gave a huge sigh. He lifted his head out of Uncle Daney's lap and sniffed along the rim of a wheel. His eyes looked faraway and thoughtful.

Then he shook his head and lumbered off, one big hoof at a time, toward the pile of logs where the young steer was standing. The steer looked astonished, stuck his tail straight in the air, and galloped away.

"Never seen a horse before?" Uncle Daney cackled. He started to turn his chair again and paused. "You'd have a lot more pasture, Bill," he said, "if you'd pull out some of them junipers."

Stewie had unloaded more things while they were putting Nip out to pasture. There was a pile of dark, dusty leather beside Uncle Daney's stall, a huge leather collar hanging on a nail, and strange pieces of wood: curved ones with brass knobs on the ends, a straight piece with iron rings.

Pop opened the stall door. "We took your suggestion, Daney. Hope it's all right. . . ." Now Pop sounded a little nervous.

Uncle Daney rolled over the threshold that Cole and Pop had worked so hard to make smooth. He stopped in the center of the stall and looked around for a long moment. They could see only the back of his head. Mom pressed her lips together and reached for Pop's hand.

"Would you rather be in the trailer with us, Uncle Daney? We can—"

Uncle Daney shook his head. When he spoke, he sounded as if he'd taken his teeth out again. "I never had a place as nice as this, Lou." He wheeled himself over to the bed. Cole watched the tires roll smoothly across the sanded floor. The bed was the same height as the chair, and Uncle Daney could slip onto it without help. He straightened out his thin, motionless legs with his hands and then lay back against the pillow. He watched while Pop showed him how the gas heater worked and where everything was. Then he said, "Thank you, Bill. Thank you, Lou." There was nothing more, but his words were like gifts.

Cole was pleased when Pop said, "Cole did most of the work."

"Did, did he?" Uncle Daney looked at Cole, and Cole hastily drew his brows down in a frown. Uncle Daney smiled. "Just like your grandfather," he said. "He always looked at me just that way!" Everybody started to look at Cole, but Uncle Daney's voice caught them quickly.

"Guess I'll catch forty winks, if you don't mind. Stewie—"

Stewie stepped forward. He had to stoop a little, and he took up most of the stall. He reached down and shook Uncle Daney's hand. "Be seein' ya, Daney," he rumbled, and turned away. His huge whiskery face was red and sad.

"Don't do anything I wouldn't do," Uncle Daney called after him.

Then he relaxed against the pillow. Cole wondered why Uncle Daney had gone to bed right away like that. An old, crippled man who had just ridden a long way in a truck might be worn out. But Uncle Daney's eyes were bright, and the way he lay against the pillow, looking around the stall, Cole didn't think he was planning on going to sleep just yet.

*   *   *

When Uncle Daney had unpacked, the stall didn't seem any fuller. He didn't own anything, as far as Cole could tell, except Nip, and work clothes, and a lot of long underwear.

The rest of the weekend Cole and Pop cut wood, and the only thing different was that when Cole looked up, there was a big red horse out among the junipers. Every time Cole saw Nip, he felt a little jolt of surprise. It was the same surprise he felt each time he saw Uncle Daney in the wheelchair, sitting in the big doorway of the barn. The wheelchair was what he'd expected, but Uncle Daney was not.

They all ate supper together on Sunday night. Lingering over dessert, when Pop had gone back to the house, Cole learned surprising things. He'd known Mom was the one who most wanted them to own their own land, but he hadn't known why.

"I watched my father work all his life at a job he hated," Mom told Uncle Daney. "I didn't want Bill getting bitter like Dad did."

Cole learned that Mom was worried because now they had their own land it seemed as if Pop worked harder than ever.

He learned that she was worried about *him*. "Even Cole works too hard," she said. "And he hasn't made friends here."

What about you? Cole thought. None of them had

made friends yet, and Mom spent all day sitting in the trailer, sewing doll dresses for a nearby factory to make a little extra money.

"I'm not complaining," Mom said. "It's just nice having family around to talk to."

"Never spent much time with family," Uncle Daney said thoughtfully. "Hit out for the log camps when I was sixteen." To Cole he didn't sound regretful. He sounded pleased with where he'd been and pleased with where he was now.

"What was it like, Uncle Daney?" Mom asked. She looked like a little girl asking for a story.

Uncle Daney sat thinking. His eyes got larger and brighter, but secret-looking, as if he had much he couldn't tell. After a minute he said, "Cole, there's an envelope in that table by the bed. Get it for me?"

Cole brought the envelope. It was brown and cracked, and inside he could see a few curled black-and-white snapshots. Uncle Daney took them out and handed them to Mom. "This is me," he said. "Young feller that worked with us one summer sent 'em to me. That was back in— 'thirty-nine, I guess."

Cole looked over Mom's shoulder at the pictures.

An enormous load of logs, pulled by six horses. High on the logs perched a thin teenaged boy, his hair flying straight up like a tongue of flame.

A bunkhouse, dirty-looking in the black and white of the picture. There was deeply rutted mud in front of the door and a white dog scratching itself. Three men and the thin boy sat on the step playing cards.

Two huge men and the boy with the wild hair, dancing some kind of jig for the camera. The men danced heavily, and their grins were bashful. The boy, between them, had linked his arms through theirs, and he was kicking up his heels. His legs looked so loose and limber Cole almost expected to see them move. The other two were stopped in time, but the little one was still dancing. Cole kept himself from looking across the table at Uncle Daney in the wheelchair.

Mom looked up from the pictures. "You had fun, didn't you? I always thought you must have."

Uncle Daney's eyes gleamed. He loosened his teeth—both sets—rotated them in his mouth, and settled them into place again. "Ay-yup," he said. "I did."

On Monday, when Cole got off the bus, Uncle Daney was sitting alone outside his stall, looking at the big heap of leather that Stewie had dropped there. He waved, but not as if he expected Cole to come over.

Normally Cole would have gone inside for a glass of milk and a snack, and then, with nothing else to do, he'd have hiked up to the top of the Hogback. But it didn't seem right to walk past Uncle Daney without stopping to say hello.

"What you doing?"

"Figurin'," said Uncle Daney. He didn't look up.

"Figuring what?"

"Ropes. Pulleys. Know anything about pulleys?" He glanced up in his sharp way, and Cole nodded cautiously.

"Got any?"

"There's some around," Cole admitted. "How big?"

"How big'd they need to be to lift this harness up there?" Uncle Daney pointed to the rafters that crossed above the aisle.

Now Cole knew he was being strung along, but he couldn't help asking, "What you want to do that for?"

"You don't think I'm in any shape to lift a harness by myself, do you?" Uncle Daney cackled. "Heh! Never was big enough! Neither are you."

"But what do you want to lift it for?"

"You wouldn't be a bad-lookin' boy if you'd quit aglowerin'!" Uncle Daney said. "How am I gonna get the danged thing onto Nip if I don't lift it?"

The job took most of the week, and all the pulleys Cole could find, in the toolboxes, from the old block and tackle, and rusting in back corners of the barn. For rope, Uncle Daney braided baling twine; all day long, Cole thought. Every afternoon when Cole got off the bus, Uncle Daney had what seemed like another fifty feet, neatly coiled beside his chair.

Friday, when he got home, the visiting nurse was

there. Mom had been dreading that. "Even way out here," she said, "you can't stick an old man out in a barn without somebody getting upset about it!"

But the visiting nurse was charmed. "It's ideal," she said to Mom. "So many old people want the independence he has. It's so hard never being alone and always acting like a guest." As she got into her car, she added, "But if I were you, I'd move the whole family out there! What a great house that barn would make!"

"Someday we may do that," Mom said.

When the nurse was gone, Cole laid the harness out in the aisle. It was heavy and stiff, and he had to haul instead of lift it.

Uncle Daney wheeled all the way around the harness, scratching thoughtfully at the stubble on his chin. Then he showed Cole where to attach the ropes and how to tie quick-release knots, which came loose with one tug. "Think that'll do it," he said. "Back in the camps I had it rigged so's I could do it anywhere there was a good strong tree limb. Didn't often have a barn as good as this to work in."

Cole got out the tall stepladder and threaded all the ropes through the pulleys, brought them together, and spliced them into the main rope, which ran down to a cleat near the door.

When they were ready, Uncle Daney wheeled himself slowly out by the door. He took hold of the main rope and pulled it, hand over hand. The huge, heavy harness lifted up silently. The ropes spread it wide, so that Cole could almost see a horse shape within it. Uncle Daney hoisted it straight to the beams. Then he lowered it again, to the height of Nip's back.

"Works pretty slick," he said to Cole. "Want to try her?"

Cole was amazed at how easy it was. The harness seemed to weigh nothing at all.

He was just wrapping the rope around the cleat when Mom came out, bringing Uncle Daney's supper. She stared up at the beams, and Uncle Daney said, "Got that danged old thing hung up out of your way, Lou. Mmm, that smells good!"

On the weekend Pop tilled the pea patch. He had a huge, rusty old Rototiller that had been in the barn when they bought this place. It was as noisy as the chain saw, and it shook Pop all over, so hard that his hat fell off. Uncle Daney came out to watch. Once, after the tiller had stalled, Cole heard Pop ask, "That horse know how to pull a plow, Daney?"

"He never has," said Uncle Daney, "but that don't mean we can't teach him."

But that was all Uncle Daney said about Nip all weekend. He wheeled out to the gate once. Nip came and leaned over the bars, and Uncle Daney spent half an hour with him. After Uncle Daney had come back, Cole took a rake and smoothed the humps of grass near the gate and pushed the stones aside.

"Glad you did that, Cole," Pop said later. "He seems pretty attached to that horse. Like him to be able to spend time with him as long as he's here."

"Is Uncle Daney going somewhere?"

"No, but the horse has to," Pop said regretfully. "We've got just about enough grass for the one beef critter."

"We could feed him hay," Cole said. He hadn't socialized with Nip yet, but he liked the way the horse looked, big and blond among the dark junipers.

"Hay costs," said Pop. "Even with Daney giving us what's left of his government check, there's still hospital bills, and fixing his place up set me back quite a little. I don't see how I can do it, Cole."

Cole didn't see either when Pop put it that way. But he knew that giving up Nip wasn't in Uncle Daney's plans. For a minute he thought he should tell Pop about the harness in the rafters. Then he decided it was better just to wait and see.

|| CHAPTER THREE ||

ON MONDAY AFTERNOON, when Cole got off the bus, Uncle Daney was waiting. Nip's halter was in his hand.

"Open the gate for me, Cole," he said, crunching slowly toward the pasture.

Suddenly Cole felt impatient. "Want to get there a little quicker?" he asked, and without waiting for an answer, he grabbed the two handles of the wheelchair and started running. Uncle Daney was heavier than he looked, and Cole had to push hard. The wheelchair bumped over a stone, and Uncle Daney let out a yelp. Then he started to cackle, high-pitched and breathless.

"Wheee! Chariot ride! Heh-heh-heh!" It took him a minute, at the gate, to catch his breath. Then he whistled once, between his teeth. Out among the junipers Nip lifted his head and stared.

Uncle Daney whistled again. Slowly Nip turned and picked his way through the junipers toward them.

"Head down," Uncle Daney told him. He buckled on the halter and wheeled himself out through the gate.

Back at the barn Uncle Daney led Nip inside. He turned him around to face out the big door, and he dropped the rope.

"Don't you want to tie him?" Cole asked.

"He's ground-tied. He won't move till I pick up that rope."

"He can move any time he wants to!" Cole said.

"That may be true, but he don't know it. That's trainin', boy. That's how you handle a horse. Muscle won't get you nowhere, even if you're as big as Stewie. Now get me them brushes, there in the grain bag. Always brush a horse before you put leather on him." Uncle Daney paused and cackled. "Course, things being what they are, you'll have to do it. I can't reach much farther than his belly."

Even Cole couldn't reach everywhere. He had to stand on a crate to brush Nip's broad back.

Cole had seen big horses like this at the pulling contests. They pranced to the stoneboat—a heavy prance, harness jingling. They turned; they lunged forward, sometimes even before they were hitched. It could take three big men, all working hard, to hitch a team to a stoneboat.

But Nip didn't seem to be like that, at least not now.

He stood quietly, staring straight ahead in his mild, thoughtful way, while Cole brushed his back and sides and Uncle Daney brushed his legs.

"Now his feet. Always check a horse's feet before you use him."

Were they going to use Nip? And for what?

And how on earth was Cole supposed to pick up those feet, which were bigger than dinner plates?

"Give a little pull on the long hair there," Uncle Daney said, "so he knows which foot you want. And say, 'Give me your foot.' "

Before Cole could move, Nip lifted one front foot and stood holding it up.

Uncle Daney wheeled a little closer. "Looks nice and clean," he said. "Do the rest, Cole, and I'll keep quiet. He'll need to get used to you talkin' to him."

A sudden shiver went down Cole's back. He had a feeling he was getting into something, maybe deeper than he wanted. Or was it that he'd gotten in already, without realizing? He moved to Nip's back leg and said, "Give me your foot, Nip."

Nip turned his head and looked back at Cole.

"Give me your foot."

Nip turned to look straight ahead again. In a slow, patient way, he picked up his back foot.

"Hey! He understood!"

"Course he understood," said Uncle Daney. "Is his foot clean?"

When Cole had checked all of Nip's feet, it was time to try lowering the harness.

"You let me do it," Uncle Daney said, "and you stay back. It's been awhile; this might startle him."

"I could get out of the way quicker than you," said Cole.

"Maybe so, but he don't know you. Step back." Uncle Daney wheeled up to the cleat and unwound the rope. "Easy, Nip," he said. "Easy, Nip." His voice was gentle and calming, as the harness started to come down.

Suddenly Nip saw it. He threw up his head, the quickest move Cole had yet seen him make, and he started to take a step.

"Whoa!"

Uncle Daney's voice was like a steel bar, dropped in front of Nip's chest. The big horse stopped abruptly, still looking tense, but as if moving were impossible.

"Good boy!" The harness settled on Nip's back, and Uncle Daney let it rest on him a minute. Then he said, "Easy, Nip," and lifted it. Up and down he moved the harness, until Nip relaxed and lowered his head.

"All right, that's enough for today." Uncle Daney said. "Tomorrow we'll drive him."

The next day, when Cole got home, Uncle Daney had Nip out in the yard.

"I'll be right there!" Cole yelled, running toward the trailer.

Inside, Mom looked up from her sewing. "Cookies on the table," she said. "Take some out to your uncle Daney."

"How'd he get Nip out?" Cole asked.

"He just went out and did it," said Mom. "And then he spent all day sitting out there with him, beside the road. He said he wanted to give Nip some better grass, but see if you can find out what he's up to."

But Uncle Daney gave Cole no chance to ask questions. It was time to learn about harnessing. Cole stood on a box to slide the big leather collar over Nip's head and settle it on his shoulders. He lowered the harness. He put the long, curved wooden pieces with the brass knobs on the end, the hames, into the grooves on the collar, and buckled them tight. He fastened the buckles on the harness. Then Uncle Daney handed him the bridle.

"Tell him, 'Head down,' " said Uncle Daney, and before Cole could say anything, Nip lowered his head. "Hold the top of the bridle in your right hand and the bit in your left," Uncle Daney said, "and stick your thumb in the corner of his mouth. Tell him, 'Open up.' "

Nip opened his jaws. There was a slight sound as he did, and Cole saw the horse's huge yellow teeth. They passed his fingers and closed around the bit, and then Nip settled it back in his mouth, with the same motion Uncle Daney used when he put in his teeth.

"Get his ears in," Uncle Daney advised, and quickly

Cole stuffed them through the openings in the top of the bridle.

"Good," said Uncle Daney. "Now we can start teachin' you to drive."

"Where are the reins?" Cole asked, looking around. He didn't see any more leather anywhere. All of it seemed to be on Nip.

"I don't use reins on him," Uncle Daney said. "Don't know why I bother with the bridle. Looks, I guess."

"But—"

"We'll take him out on the driveway," said Uncle Daney, wheeling himself over the threshold onto the gravel. "Nip, walk." Slowly, foot by heavy foot, Nip followed Uncle Daney out onto the driveway.

When Uncle Daney was in the widest part, between the barn and the trailer, he stopped his chair. Nip hesitated.

"Walk on, Nip."

Nip put his ears out to the sides, as if he was of two minds about this, but he kept on walking. He was heading straight toward the plowed and seeded pea patch. Cole opened his mouth to say something, but he kept the words from coming out. He saw his mother, sewing by the window, look up. Then she vanished, and a moment later she was looking out the door.

When Nip was about ten feet from the pea patch, Uncle Daney said quietly, "Nip, haw."

Nip turned, and when he had made a perfect right

angle, Uncle Daney said, "Walk on." Nip started walking straight again, heading down the driveway.

"You see?" said Uncle Daney. " 'Twas horses like him made a logger out of me. I wan't never the right size to be one on my own. Haw, Nip. Now walk on."

Uncle Daney drove Nip around him in a perfect square, and then he said, "Whoa." Nip stopped, once again as if a bar had dropped in front of him. "Now *you* take the reins," Uncle Daney said, looking up at Cole.

Cole waited.

"You remember the words." Uncle Daney dropped his voice. " 'Walk' means forward, 'haw' is left, 'gee' is right, and 'whoa' is whoa. Take him in a square, like I done."

Cole swallowed. "All right. Nip, walk."

Nip looked around at Cole and Uncle Daney, his ears pricked gently forward.

"Again," said Uncle Daney.

"Nip, walk."

This time Cole's voice sounded firmer. Nip gave a big sigh and started walking forward. He was heading straight toward the pea patch again, and getting closer.

"Um—gee, Nip! Gee! I mean—" Nip promptly and obligingly turned right, straight toward the trailer. He stopped with his head over the railing around the little front stoop.

Mom opened the door and came out. "Hello, Nip," she said softly. Nip pricked his ears at her. "Uncle Daney, I have an apple core. Can he have it?"

"Go ahead and give it to him," Uncle Daney said. "Now, Cole, when she finishes, you'll tell him, 'Back up.' When he's clear of the railing, you'll gee him again, and then you'll straighten him out." He didn't look up, and Cole felt the red gradually going out of his face. He waited until Nip was through crunching the apple core, and then he said, "Nip, back up!" It went as easily as it had sounded.

"It's like a remote-controlled race car," Cole said when he had driven Nip in four or five squares around them.

"What's that?" asked Uncle Daney.

"It's a car you can steer from far away."

"Really? Always figured you had to be right *in* a car— any car I ever heard of!"

"No, it's a toy. Oh—um . . . gee, Nip. Okay, walk. I'll show you after."

"Might's well show me now," Uncle Daney said. "We'll put him away, and you go get it."

When Pop came home at dusk, the two of them were still outside, playing with the little red car.

|| CHAPTER FOUR ||

FOR THE NEXT two afternoons Cole drove Nip in the yard, learning to make sharp and wide angles, diagonals and zigzags.

During the days Uncle Daney sat with Nip by the side of the road. Old men were beginning to stop and talk with him, Mom said, old men driving trucks, old men in work pants and suspenders.

Thursday night Cole heard Pop say, "I don't know what to do about it, Lou. He's a wily old bird, and he's getting Cole attached to that horse. But you know we can't afford to keep him."

"Uncle Daney has his ways," Mom said. "I know Dad always said to watch out . . ." She said more, but she dropped her voice, and Cole couldn't quite catch it. That was the worst thing about the trailer. He was always hearing a little more than he wanted to hear, or a little less.

Friday, when Cole got off the bus, an old man with a big team of dappled gray horses was plowing the rest of the garden. Uncle Daney sat out next to the pea patch, watching. He and the other man shouted back and forth to each other. The man's harness was rich-looking, bright with brass.

Cole walked out along the furrows to where Uncle Daney sat. He could see the first pale, bent pea sprouts pushing up. "Who's that, Uncle Daney?"

"Ray West. Lives up the road a piece."

"So how come he's plowing our garden?"

"Sit by a road long enough," Uncle Daney said, "and everything you need'll come by."

"Oh." Cole watched the big gray horses walking slow and straight across the garden patch, the fat old man on the brightly painted riding plow. It wasn't the kind of thing he'd ever seen come down the road before. There's more to it, he thought.

"Nope, you can't pay me," Ray West told Pop. He had just loaded the big gray horses into his truck when Pop got back from the mill. "Needed to get set for the plowin' contests, and m'wife won't let me have any more lawn. I was glad when Daney offered me the chance."

"Maybe Ray West would take Nip," Pop said that weekend, as he and Cole worked on the wood. "There's enough grass now, but come July there won't be. I just hope Daney'll see that without me having to say anything. Hate like heck to hurt the old cuss's feelings."

Cole didn't answer. Pop didn't know much about Uncle Daney, he was starting to realize. Cole didn't either, but at least he knew to expect surprises.

There was no school Monday or for the rest of that week—spring vacation. As soon as breakfast was done Monday morning, Uncle Daney said, "Run out and catch up Nip for me, young un."

Cole figured Uncle Daney might want to get an early start on his roadside sitting, though it seemed strange he didn't go get Nip himself. He took the big halter and went out and whistled Uncle Daney's low, flat whistle. It was nice to see Nip out among the junipers, turning and lumbering toward him. Nip seemed surprised, when he got up close, to see that the whistler was not Uncle Daney. But when Cole spoke, he lowered his head patiently to be haltered.

Back at the barn Uncle Daney was waiting, tapping his fingers on his chair.

"Are you taking him out by the road today?" Cole asked.

"What would I do that for? Bring him here, young un! Brush him down!"

Quickly Cole brushed Nip's upper reaches and then checked his hooves.

"Now harness him up," said Uncle Daney. "Want to see if you remember how."

Cole got the collar off the wall, sneaking a look at Uncle Daney as he did. It made him feel uneasy that Uncle Daney was sitting back like this, not doing things. But the old man seemed as healthy as ever, and his blue eyes were bright.

When the harness was on, Uncle Daney reached to the wall beside him and took down a piece of wood hanging there. It had an iron ring and hook in the middle and smaller rings on each end, with chains looped through them. Uncle Daney handed the piece of wood to Cole.

"This here's the whippletree," he said. "Hook it on to the tugs, there."

The tugs were the long, thick straps that ran back from Nip's collar. They ended in iron hooks, and until now they had been looped up and hanging from rings at the back of the harness. Cole took them down and caught the hooks securely into the loops of chain on the ends of the whippletree.

"Now this," Uncle Daney said. He handed Cole a long, heavy chain with a hook on each end. It was rust-colored but strong-looking. "Hook it on to the whippletree," Uncle Daney said. "Nope, put the two hooks together, Cole, and let the chain trail. That way it won't catch on anything. Now get me them brush clippers I seen you usin' Saturday."

"What for?"

"Because I asked you to!" Uncle Daney looked impish. Cole felt like balking. He could refuse to take another step till Uncle Daney explained. The trouble was, Uncle Daney would probably balk, too. He got the brush clippers, and Uncle Daney took them on his lap.

"One more thing," he said, handing Cole two plastic bread bags. "G'wan up there in the mow and fill these with chaff."

Cole did as he was told. He felt like the kid who gets invited up from the audience to be made a fool of by the magician, but he didn't see what choice he had. He gave the full bags to Uncle Daney, who tucked them beside him in the chair.

"All right," he said, "let's go. Give me a push, Cole, will you?"

Now Cole did ask, "Are you feeling okay?"

"Ay-yup! Just don't want to get all tuckered out before we even start."

Start what? Cole took hold of the wheelchair handles. He looked down at the top of Uncle Daney's head. "Where are we going?"

"Out to the back pasture," Uncle Daney said. "Nip, walk."

The chair rolled pretty smoothly up to the barway. Cole got Uncle Daney through it, and he closed it behind Nip. Nip kept walking where Uncle Daney guided him, and

Cole watched the whippletree bump over the grass, clanking and jingling a little. The long chain followed like a snake.

Then he took hold of the chair again and followed Nip, out along the winding fence line. It was much harder going here. The little front wheels turned every time they hit a bump, and the grass seemed to hold them back. Uncle Daney helped whenever Cole stalled, and when he did, Cole could feel how strong he was, how strong he *had* to be, to move himself around. A sharp smell of sweat came up from him, and Cole realized Mom hadn't been bossing Uncle Daney hard enough. He seemed to have been wearing this shirt a few days too many.

Now the pasture took a big swoop around the Hogback, out of sight of the trailer. It was smoother going here. Uncle Daney sat back, looking around at the grass, the dark junipers, and the huge, arching wild roses, then tipping his head back to look up the Hogback. Nip paused. "Walk on," Uncle Daney said.

"How far are we going?" Cole asked.

"Gettin' tired?"

"No."

"All the way," Uncle Daney said, pointing at the back fence.

When they reached the fence, Uncle Daney stopped Nip, and he turned his chair around to face the way they'd come.

The junipers were thinner out here, and smaller. Uncle Daney pointed to the nearest one, a low, prickly cushion that spread almost as wide as his chair. "That un first," he said.

Cole wasn't going to ask—he just *wasn't*! He looked from the juniper to Nip, the whippletree, the chain. He took the chain off the whippletree, knelt on the warm spring ground, and started to wrap the chain around the bush.

"Lower down, I should think," Uncle Daney said, "and maybe a little tighter."

Cole reached in farther under the juniper and found its main trunk. It was surprisingly slender—not much bigger around than a broomstick. He hooked the chain tight.

"All right, now straighten out that chain, and bring Nip around to the end of it. Pick up the whippletree, so it don't catch on something."

Cole picked up the whippletree by the hook. "Walk, Nip. Gee." The whippletree bounced with Nip's slow steps. Cole was close to Nip's red haunches and his blond tail, close enough to remember how much they had to trust Nip never to kick, never to run away. "Whoa." Nip stopped at the end of the chain. Cole put the whippletree on the ground, and he hooked the long chain to it.

"Now, Cole," said Uncle Daney, "slide under the back side of that juniper, and cut where you see the roots go down into the ground—just on that side. Then you step back, and I'll give Nip the word, and we'll see if we can tip 'er up some. Maybe you'll have to jump in and do some more cuttin'. All right?" He handed Cole the brush clippers.

Cole had his doubts. He could see himself sliding under the tipped-up juniper and having it close on his head like a clam. How was Uncle Daney going to tell Nip not to back off the pressure? And what if the juniper scared Nip?

But he kept this to himself, got down on knees and elbows, and snaked in under the low, prickly branches.

It was a small bush, but tough. At this awkward angle it was a struggle to make the clippers bite into the wood. One, two, three places he cut, where the strong roots came up out of the earth. He made sure the chain was snug around the trunk and then slithered out again.

Uncle Daney said, "All right, Nip. Walk." Two steps. The chain stretched straight and taut, and Uncle Daney said, *"Hup!"* There was a creaking sound of leather as Nip leaned his weight into the collar, a tearing sound from underneath the juniper bush. Nip kept going without a pause, and the juniper turned upside down, roots splayed to the sun. The little balls and crumbles of dirt were still falling when Uncle Daney said, "Whoa!"

Cole unhooked the chain from the juniper. Most of the shallow, spreading roots were split or broken. There were only a couple to cut. He lifted up the juniper like a trophy, like a big string of fish.

"Worked pretty slick," said Uncle Daney. "Well, that was a little un. We'll see."

"What should I do with it?"

"Shake the dirt off," Uncle Daney said, "and put it somewheres where we can start a pile." As he spoke, he struggled out of his flannel shirt. The sun shone on his bare arms, white and skinny and roped with muscle. Then he made a cud-chewing motion and swept his false teeth out of his mouth. He handed the set to Cole.

"Stick them danged things on top of a fence post, will you? Now let's get down to work!"

Cole turned from the wet grin of Uncle Daney's choppers on the post and looked back across the pasture. Just in this section, before it took that curve around the bottom of the Hogback, there were hundreds of junipers.

He looked down at the little patch of bare ground they had just made. Already the crumbles of dirt were turning gray in the sun. Uncle Daney reached into one of the breadbags and tossed a handful of chaff onto the bare spot.

"Just step on that once, Cole, tread it in a little."

Cole obeyed, but he couldn't help saying, "It won't grow fast enough, you know. Even if we clear the whole pasture, we can't make enough grass for Nip."

"Well, not *this* summer," Uncle Daney said.

They worked all morning, and by the time Mom came out to find them, Cole knew he was having fun.

They all were sweating in the spring sunshine. Sweat trickled down from under Nip's collar and darkened the places where the harness straps rested on his back. Uncle Daney's sleeveless undershirt clung to his body. Cole wasn't wearing any shirt at all now. The knees of his pants were stiff and shiny with dirt, molded in the shape of his kneecaps, and he had dirt all over his chest and arms. Juniper needles kept falling out of his hair.

They had popped seven junipers out of the ground. They had seen a bluebird and three circling hawks. It was quiet. Just the creak of harness, the ripping sound of roots coming out of the ground, sometimes Uncle Daney's high-pitched cackle and his instructions, toothless and mushy, but understandable.

Then Nip lifted his head and pointed his ears. Cole and Uncle Daney looked, too, and there was Mom coming across the pasture.

"Uh-oh!" Uncle Daney said. "Here's where we catch it!"

Cole thought so, too. He waited, watching Mom come nearer. She looked like Uncle Daney, he thought: small and wiry, with that same wispy hair and that same way of holding up her head.

"Cole! Uncle Daney! What are you two up to?"

"Clearin' you some pastureland, Lou."

"I can't understand a word you're saying!" Mom said crossly. She spotted the teeth grinning on the fence post, brought them over, and handed them to Uncle Daney.

"I should think you could *see* what we're doin'," Uncle Daney said, speaking clearly again.

Mon looked back across the low, dark sea of junipers. "All I can say is you've tackled an almighty big job!"

"Some feller cleared it afore our time," Uncle Daney said. "If he could, I guess we can!"

Mom looked down at him, and Cole could tell that for a second she was seeing the chair, though that normally wasn't what you saw when you looked at Uncle Daney. She smiled faintly and shook her head.

"I'd look on it as a favor if you wouldn't mention this to Bill," Uncle Daney said. "He'll notice once we get around this bend, but I'd like to keep it a surprise."

Mom didn't believe they ever would get around the bend, and Cole couldn't blame her. He kept himself from looking back across the pasture, because every time he did, he started counting.

"All right," Mom said. "But, Cole, you wear your oldest pants from now on—and come Saturday, I'm going to teach you a few things about laundry! Now come on in, you two—you *three*! It's time for lunch."

That was the shortest spring break Cole had ever had. Every day, morning and afternoon, they spent out back, skinning junipers out of the ground, sprinkling chaff on the torn earth. It got so that Cole saw junipers every time he closed his eyes. Junipers were all he could think about, and he hated to quit at lunchtime or in the evening. It was like picking berries. He always wanted just one more.

They cleared out the smallest junipers, all the way to the bend. Then they went back for the middle-size ones, and then it was Friday. There were some huge bushes left, and where the pasture climbed a little way up the shoulder of the Hogback there were more, all sizes.

"We'll have to leave 'em," Uncle Daney said. "I can't roll this contraption up there to help." He popped his teeth back in his mouth and swirled them into place, looking down glumly at the muddy wheels of his chair.

"Guess I could get them by myself," Cole said. He waited for Uncle Daney's reaction.

Uncle Daney looked from him to Nip, standing near them with his eyes half-closed. After a minute he said, "Ay-yup, I guess likely you could."

Saturday it rained hard, too hard even for Pop, who hardly ever let weather stop him from working.

But this Saturday Pop splashed across to the barn and played checkers with Uncle Daney. Mom and Cole went to the Laundromat.

When Cole was little, he always used to go with Mom to wash clothes on rainy Saturdays. He liked the smell of soap and clean clothes, the sound of the washers and dryers whirling. He liked the lazy, bored talk all around him. And he liked being with Mom, even if she was making him learn how to take dirt stains out of blue jeans.

"How's it going out in the juniper patch?" she asked.

Cole explained how far they'd gotten. There was a huge pile of junipers waiting to be burned, sometime after they'd told Pop.

"And you don't mind, Cole, that you're the one doing all the work for this great project?"

Cole stared at her. That was something he'd never thought about. Now that he did think of it, it didn't seem true. Uncle Daney was out there every minute, sweating and swearing, driving him and Nip like a team. "I don't do *all* the work," he said. "Besides, Uncle Daney thought of it."

Mom laughed, biting her lip as if she was trying to stop herself. "Oh, Cole. Uncle Daney's always had his ways of getting things done. That's what used to make your grandfather so mad. He worked hard all his life at a job he hated, and Daney did what he felt like doing and was happy."

"Uncle Daney worked hard all *his* life, too," Cole said.

Mom said, "The difference is it was Uncle Daney's choice. Poor Dad always felt like *he'd* been backed into a corner in life."

"Was he?"

"No," Mom said. "He chose, too. The real difference is that Uncle Daney always lands right side up. Even now. He doesn't own anything in the world but the clothes on his back and that horse—" Mom shook her head and smiled helplessly. "And Dad died with a house and a car and money in the bank. And to his dying day he thought Daney had a better deal in life!"

"Do *you* think so?" Cole asked after a minute.

"Oh, yes!" Mom said.

|| CHAPTER FIVE ||

In school on Monday Cole was one of the three or four people with dark spring tans. "Where did *you* go?" people in homeroom kept asking all of them.

"Florida," said Brie Alexander, with a little shake of her head that set her gold earrings trembling. "It was *so* boring!" And Mark had been to Bermuda and said he had a tan all over.

Only Cole knew that his was a farmer's tan—top half only. He wanted to say he'd been somewhere, but when Brie asked, he couldn't think of any place, and he felt his face get red. "Oh, I was just pulling junipers in the back pasture," he said. His voice sounded old-time and farmerish to him, different from other people's. "Me and my uncle and his horse."

Brie turned away, hunching her shoulder. *So* boring.

But Roger Allard stopped leg wrestling with Jason a minute later and came over. He was tanned, too, but nobody asked where he'd been, Cole had noticed. "Your family works with horses?" Roger asked.

"Well . . . my uncle does."

"My father and my uncles have a big cordwood operation," Roger said. "We have eight or ten teams working most of the time."

"Do *you* drive one?"

Roger nodded. "Oh, yeah!" He flexed his arm, and a big muscle popped up. "Takes all I got to hold 'em sometimes. Better than lifting weights!"

"Oh." Cole wanted to look down at his own muscle, but he didn't think snipping juniper roots with a pair of brush clippers had built him up much. "My uncle's horse is pretty old," he said. Then the bell rang. Cole took his seat at the back corner of the room, and Roger went to sit with his friends again.

That week Cole took Nip up the shoulder of the Hogback and got all the small and medium-size junipers. Uncle Daney sat on the flat below and watched, but he didn't say much. At first Cole felt bad about that, as if he were eating a candy bar in front of a hungry little kid. But Uncle Daney didn't seem to feel bad, and after a while Cole began to enjoy himself, up there on the hillside alone with Nip. His voice sounded crisper and surer, and Nip responded almost as quickly as he did to Uncle Daney.

Nip was in good shape now. Long, smooth muscles creased his haunches. Veins stood out on his legs and belly. Even his coat seemed brighter with the work. He was ready to come back to level ground and tackle the big junipers, Uncle Daney said.

Cole wondered. The first bush they tackled was almost as wide as Mom and Pop's trailer. He had to crawl a long way to find the roots, and then they were too big to cut with the brush clippers. He had to run all the way back to the barn and get a saw.

After he'd cut the first few roots, he backed out, and Uncle Daney said, *"Hup!"* Nip hit the collar hard. The whole harness creaked loudly, and for a moment nothing seemed to happen. Then something popped under the juniper, and it gave a little. "All right," Uncle Daney said, and Nip eased off the pressure. "Slide in under there, Cole, and see if you can cut some more."

More roots were exposed now. Cole sawed, Nip pulled again, Cole cut again, and finally, with a great tearing sound, the juniper came out of the ground. Uncle Daney let Nip drag it about fifty feet before he stopped him. "Gotta let him feel like he's gettin' somewhere. Bad for a horse to let him get set like that."

"What does that mean?"

"Tryin' to pull somethin' he can't budge. Gets him discouraged. If it happens too much, he'll quit tryin'."

Cole looked at Nip, standing where Uncle Daney had stopped him. Even at this distance he could see Nip's sides heave. The juniper behind him looked like a crouching black bear.

"Should we keep him at it?" he asked, looking around at the dark, spreading monster junipers.

"I dunno." Uncle Daney rasped a hand over his stubbly chin. "Might see if Ray West—uh-oh! The jig's up!"

Cole looked, and there was Pop, walking along the pasture fence. They had been working so hard on the big juniper they'd forgotten the time.

Pop was walking slowly, and now he stopped. He looked at the patches of bare dirt, some with a pale green fuzz of grass sprouts starting. He looked at the two big piles of junipers, both higher than Cole's head. And he looked at Nip, and Cole, and Uncle Daney. He took his cap off and scratched the back of his head, and then he came over.

"How far do you figure to take this project?" he asked.

"All the way!" said Uncle Daney. "Only thing is, I don't know about them rosebushes. Can't get close enough to wrap a chain around 'em."

Pop looked back across the pasture. "If you just get the junipers, we'll be most of the way there. Rosebushes don't amount to much."

"Might burn 'em," Uncle Daney said with an eager gleam in his eye. Cole could just see him, dousing a rosebush with kerosene and starting a fire that would burn off the whole Hogback.

"That might do it," Pop said. He stood for a moment,

looking around at the strangely open, blotchy pasture. "Seems a heck of a lot bigger," he said. "Well, supper's on. Daney, you want a push back?"

"Nope. We'll be along in a minute," Uncle Daney said. "Bring Nip back over here, Cole, and we'll unhitch him from that juniper."

Together Pop and Cole walked toward Nip, standing with his head down, waiting. "It's been a big help having Nip around," Cole said, when it looked like Pop wasn't going to say it.

"I know, Cole." Pop put one hand on Nip's neck and held the other out, flat. Nip dropped his nose into Pop's palm. Then his big tongue came out, once, as he licked Pop's hand. Pop sighed.

"Help isn't money, Cole, and money's what it takes. I just hope Daney'll realize without me having to tell him." He gave Nip's neck a friendly slap and walked on toward the trailer.

After Cole had brought Nip back and they'd unhooked from the juniper, Uncle Daney said, "Give me the whippletree. Got an idea." He laid the whippletree across his lap, braced one end under the arm of the chair, and got a good grip on the other end. "Nip, walk."

Nip started, and paused, feeling the strange weight and the different angle of the tugs. He looked back. "Walk," Uncle Daney said again. Nip put his ears out to the sides, of two minds about this, and walked.

Cole felt the same way. A great idea, maybe, but he

hovered right behind the chair. He saw Uncle Daney's arms tighten and bulge, his muscles bigger than Roger Allard's.

Then the little front wheels hit a hump of ground and turned sideways. The wheelchair bucked. "Whoa!" gasped Uncle Daney, and dropped the whippletree. Nip stopped, putting his ears back.

"Worked pretty slick," Uncle Daney said when he'd caught his breath. He took hold of the wheels and started to move himself along, and Cole got behind and pushed. Nip wasn't the only one who had gotten stronger; the wheelchair went across the bumpy pasture grass much more easily than it had in the beginning. "Ought to be a way to rig her so I can just hitch on—tip her back so them front wheels don't dig in."

"What about winter?" Cole asked.

"Put runners on!" said Uncle Daney with a cackle. "Then we'll move!"

"No. I mean, hay. Pop can only afford enough hay to winter one calf—"

Uncle Daney smacked his palms down on the wheels, hard, and stopped the chair with a jerk. He twisted to look up at Cole, his eyes blazing. "I ain't askin' your pop to buy hay for this horse, young feller! He pays his own way, same as I do!" He turned and started moving again, leaving Cole behind.

Cole caught up and pushed without saying anything, listening to Nip behind them and the whippletree bumping along the ground. But as they crunched onto the gravel driveway, he couldn't help asking, "How? How can Nip earn any money?"

"When I got it figured out, sonny, I'll let ye know!" Nip's hooves thudded on the bare barn floor. Without anyone telling him, he turned around and stopped, facing out the door. His big face looked mild and thoughtful, as always.

Slowly Uncle Daney wheeled up to him. Nip dropped his head, and Uncle Daney's rough, scarred hand rubbed the white spot between Nip's eyes. "You've got a head on your shoulders, young un," Uncle Daney said after a moment. "*You* think of something!"

|| CHAPTER SIX ||

COLE THOUGHT, as spring rolled on. He knew Ray West earned prize money at the plowing contests, but those were almost through already. Besides, Nip didn't know how to pull a plow.

There was the pulling contest at the fair—big teams pulling big sleds full of stones. They won prize money— but he'd never seen a single-horse pulling contest.

They could pull junipers for hire. He and Nip and Uncle Daney knew everything about pulling junipers. But any farmer around here with a fieldful of junipers had a tractor to pull them out with if he wanted to do it. The only thing Cole could think of was pony rides, and that was so silly he didn't mention it.

They busted junipers out of the ground every afternoon all spring, and Ray West got the biggest ones with his team. By the time school was out, Cole was beginning to wonder what he'd do all summer.

"Weed," Mom told him. She and Uncle Daney were riding in with Pop, early the first morning of summer vacation, because Uncle Daney had to straighten out something about his government checks.

Cole expected to find a jungle of weeds. He hadn't paid attention to the garden all spring; he'd been too busy.

But the garden looked neat and cared for. Mom? Cole wondered. Then he noticed the thin tire tracks, down all the rows. Only the onions and the corn needed a quick hoeing, and then Cole was at loose ends again.

What had he used to do with himself before Uncle Daney came? He wandered out to the barn, looked up at the harness, hanging in the beams. Then he stood in the big doorway and looked out across the pasture at Nip, the color of an old penny; the steer; and up the Hogback, dark and looming. Where the pasture rose up its shoulder, he could make out the trail he used to walk every day after school.

He had missed the arrival of the thrushes. They were all around now, their silvery, fluting songs tumbling through the air. He had almost missed the lady's slippers. He'd come just in time for the Solomon's seal, with its foamy white spikes, and where he and Pop had cut trees last fall, the ground was light and frothy with new ferns.

There were the stacked logs, waiting for the day Pop could borrow or rent a tractor again. There were the brush piles, high and snaggly, with birds and chipmunks whisking in and out. There were the trees Pop had marked to cut next and the good-size maples that would be their sugar lot. The quiet seemed odd. Cole could hear the ghost of the chain saw's roar, hear it roaring again in the future. The grove was beautiful, but he climbed quickly above it.

From the top of the Hogback he could see a long way. He could see fields, a swamp, sun gleaming off the dome of a silo, the steeple of the church. He could see steam rising up from the river valley. That was the mill where Pop worked.

Pop needed money for a tractor and a truck before he could go into business for himself. Uncle Daney needed money so he could buy hay for Nip. But there was no money, as far as Cole could see in any direction. The only money he knew about came from the mill and from the doll factory on the other side of the valley. It seemed wrong to Cole, as he looked across the green land, that there should be no money here where it looked so rich. Soberly he walked back down the Hogback and spent the rest of the morning watching TV.

When Uncle Daney came home, Cole told him about the log pile. He wasn't quite sure why, so all he did was mention that the wood was up there, that Pop would have to wait till fall to get it down.

After lunch Uncle Daney said, "Go catch Nip, young un. Want to show you how to hitch on to a log."

Mom was taking his tray back to the trailer. She stopped and turned around. "No, Uncle Daney! One of you in a wheelchair is enough!"

"Lou," said Uncle Daney, "I got hurt 'cause some danged fool that knew better was drinkin' on the job. I'm seventy years old—"

"You're older than that!"

"Maybe. Anyways, I figger I'm living proof it can be done safely—and he'll never learn any younger."

Mom pressed her lips together. After a moment she slowly nodded. "I suppose it's no more dangerous than having him out helping his father with the chain saw."

"Less," said Uncle Daney promptly. "A chain saw hasn't got a brain, and Nip does."

There were a few logs left from the pile in the pasture. Uncle Daney explained how to wrap the chain around one. Then Cole hooked Nip on to the log and practiced all afternoon, dragging it back and forth across the pasture.

"See how tight you can turn," Uncle Daney said. "Watch the log. Stay back! That's why Nip's trained like he is, so nobody's got to go hoppin' around on the log gettin' hurt."

Soon Cole had the hang of it. He figured out his turns like geometry problems—sharp angle, wide angle, straight line between two points.

The next day he drove with the log up and down the shoulder of the Hogback. "Up there," Uncle Daney said, picking out a poplar at the top of the cleared slope. "Then figure out how to get back down again. You don't want it bangin' Nip's heels, remember, and you don't have a goldanged thing to hold her back with."

From the top of the slope Cole looked down, across the blotches of dirt and the new green fuzz of sprouting grass, to Uncle Daney waiting by the log pile. The sun shone off the wheels of the chair. Uncle Daney looked very small.

Cole laid out a path in his mind, snaking across the shoulder of the Hogback in fat, lazy curves to the bottom. And then he started down.

At first he was afraid. The log looked sharp and heavy and very close to Nip's heels. If it banged into him, Nip might start running. He could get hurt, and maybe even Cole and Uncle Daney could get hurt before it was over.

Nip was worried, too, Cole thought. He obeyed promptly and smoothly, and he never looked around anymore in that questioning way when Cole told him what to do. But his ears tipped back toward Cole and the log sharply, nervously.

Nothing bad happened. Slowly Nip's ears relaxed, and after a few times Cole's heart stopped giving that quick double thump when he told Nip, "Walk."

Ray West stopped by near lunchtime. "Figure to make

a logger out of this sprout?" he asked Uncle Daney with a wink at Cole.

"Bill's got a pile of logs up the hill there," Uncle Daney said, "and no way to get 'em down. Figured we'd save him borrowin' a tractor."

Ray West squinted up the Hogback. "A horse is better for work like that, anyway. Don't tear up the ground, like a tractor does." He glanced at Cole. "You folks got a sugar lot up there?"

"Workin' on it," Cole said. He felt good saying that— like Roger Allard talking about his father's cordwood operation.

"Well"—Ray West turned to Uncle Daney—"got a line on a cart for you if you want one."

Uncle Daney's eyes brightened, but he shook his head. "Got no money, Ray."

"This cart don't cost money. It's sittin' at my brother's place, rottin'. I'll fix it up for you if it's something you want. Got nothin' much to do with myself now the plowin' contests are over. Got to stay out of the old woman's hair somehow!"

So Ray West helped Uncle Daney into the cab of his truck, put the wheelchair in the back, and they drove away. Cole watched them go. Then he climbed the Hogback to see where he would lay out the skidding trail.

Pop didn't want to use Nip to bring the logs down. "I don't know much about horses," he said, "but I know enough to know I could get in real trouble. No, thank you, Daney."

It was a hot evening, and they were eating in the aisle outside Uncle Daney's stall, on a card table Mom had brought out. Cole heard the final note in Pop's voice, but Mom sat back, smiling into her iced tea.

"Ain't askin' ye to *use* the horse," Uncle Daney said. "Cole can do that. All you got to do is help him clear the trail. Do the chain saw work. I don't believe in boys usin' chain saws."

"What about boys skidding logs, Daney? Look at yourself!"

"Seventy-five years old!" said Uncle Daney. "Figure I'm livin' proof—"

‖ CHAPTER SEVEN ‖

ALL WEEKEND COLE and Pop worked to lay out
and clear the skidding trail. Cole had thought hard about
where to put it, to avoid the steepest slopes, to make
wide, gentle curves and yet not waste too much time
walking or too many good trees. When he was through,
he wished Uncle Daney could come check his work. But
that was impossible. Pop cut the trees and then cut the
stumps flat to the ground, while Cole cut brush. Then
there was nothing left to do but try it.

On Monday night Pop got home around six-thirty.
"Couple hours of daylight left," he said to Cole. "Let's go
see if we can bring a log down."

Cole harnessed Nip, and they started up the trail. Uncle Daney waited by the log pile. Cole looked back once.
He couldn't tell how Uncle Daney felt. Cole turned and

walked on with Nip and Pop. He felt good going up the Hogback with a job to do. But he felt mean, too, as if he'd just taken something that didn't belong to him.

When they reached the pile of logs, Pop rolled one down. Cole wrapped the chain around it. Then he brought Nip around and hitched on.

"All right, Nip. Walk."

Nip looked back, pointing his ears and the blinders of his bridle at Cole. Then he heaved a big, satisfied sigh and leaned into the collar, starting the log down the trail.

"Seems right at home," Pop said. They followed Nip and the log down the winding trail. Cole watched closely, but the log never seemed to speed up and threaten Nip's heels. So he had done all right. He was ready to speak at every turn, but Nip simply followed road. He knew what he was doing. He didn't need Cole to tell him.

When they got down to the bottom, Uncle Daney was frowning. "Why in the heck did you come down? Don't you know how to use a skiddin' horse?"

"Afraid not, Daney," said Pop, laughing. He bent down and unhooked the chain from the log.

"Go on back up with him and hook on again, and then you *stay* there. He can bring the log down by himself."

"I guess he probably could," Pop said, scratching under his cap. He looked embarrassed. "But . . . can you take the chain off the log, Daney? That looks like the weak link to me. Course, I can send Cole down, and I can chain-saw by myself, but it's easier and safer with someone else there."

Uncle Daney scratched his chin. "Don't think I can unhook in this contraption," he said. "Can't reach. I could sit on the ground, though—"

Pop shook his head. "Too dangerous. You could get stepped on, or the log could roll on you."

"Why don't we ask Mom?" Cole said. "Uncle Daney could yell, and she could come out and unhook. If she wouldn't mind."

"All right," Mom said when Pop asked her. "I'd rather have you get the wood out a little at a time than work yourself to death in November."

"Daney doesn't think it's enough, does he?" Pop asked later, coming to the door of Cole's room. "Because I can get the logs out, you know. This is a big help to me, but it isn't money in the bank."

Cole felt his face get red. Of course, it wasn't enough. He'd known that all along. And, anyway, was Pop afraid of Uncle Daney? Cole was tired of being the go-between. "He hasn't said anything to me."

"Well . . . if he does . . ."

"I'll tell him," Cole said. "Pop, can I move out to the barn for the summer? It's a lot cooler."

Pop looked surprised. "I guess you'd better ask your mother," he said. "But ask Daney first. It's his place."

Cole went out to the barn. It was dark out, and there was no light in Uncle Daney's stall. Was he asleep already?

Then Cole saw the gleam of moonlight on metal in the big barn doorway, and he smelled the smell of Uncle Daney's shirt, which he'd worn a day too long. "Hi," he said.

"Hello, young feller." Uncle Daney sat quietly. Cole stood there a moment. He heard the frogs in a far-off swamp. From the direction of the pasture he heard a thud, and he heard Nip snort.

"I think he was happy to skid a log again," Cole said, just for something to say. Then he wished he'd kept quiet.

"It's been his work," said Uncle Daney. "It's what he knows."

"You, too," Cole said. Are you sad? he wanted to ask, but he didn't quite dare.

After a moment Uncle Daney gave a faint cackle. "Just thinkin'," he said. "I started out skiddin' with the reins in both hands. Then I figured out how to let the horse do the steerin', and now I got you and Bill doin' *all* the work. I'm gettin' better at this all the time!"

"I was thinking about moving into one of the other stalls for the summer," Cole said. "Would that be okay?"

"Heck, yes!" said Uncle Daney. He gave a boisterous laugh. "Nobody to boss us out here. We could have some fun!"

*   *   *

Cole chose the stall across from Uncle Daney's. When he had cleaned it, built screen windows and doors, and moved his bed in, he decided not to do anything else. He left his posters and model spaceships in the trailer. He just wanted the big, bare wooden room for a while, the hayrack in the corner, and the rough places worn in the floor by horses' hooves.

There was no time to be bored this summer. He picked the peas for Mom, and then he and Uncle Daney shelled them. By the time all the peas were eaten or in the freezer, it was time to start on string beans.

Ray West kept coming by and taking them over to look at the cart. It had started out being a square, rough little wood wagon, with a rotten floor and rusting metal sides. Ray had torn it down to the frame and rebuilt it of new wood. There were taillights, reflectors, even directionals. Every time Cole went to see it there were other old men, sometimes two or three, tinkering, swapping yarns, or bringing valuable spare parts. They acted as if they'd known Uncle Daney for a long time.

Afternoons, to keep the pasture from getting eaten down, Uncle Daney took Nip out to graze along the roadside. Sometimes Cole went along to explore in the woods and fields. Often, when he came back to the road, a truck would be parked beside Uncle Daney, and a man in work clothes would be leaning out the window to talk.

Then Pop would come home, and he and Nip and Cole would climb the Hogback. They'd hitch on to a log, and Nip would disappear with it. Pop would start to chainsaw. They'd work about twenty minutes, and then Nip would come back. After three or four trips Nip would have a bright strip of cloth tied to the brass knobs on the hames. That was Mom's signal to come on down to supper.

After supper Cole and Uncle Daney played cards or checkers or Cole might read. Uncle Daney never did read. Cole thought maybe he couldn't. He sat and whittled or made birchbark boxes from bark Cole had cut for him. Sometimes he rolled his chair to the big doorway and sat listening to the night sounds.

"Have you thought of anything yet?" Cole asked him one night. They had been sitting out for a while, looking at the warm yellow lights in the trailer and listening to a whippoorwill.

"Not yet," Uncle Daney said. "You?"

"We could give rides in the cart when it's finished."

Uncle Daney said, "It'll take a couple hundred dollars' worth of hay to feed that horse. That's a lot of cart rides."

"We could do it, though. Take him to the fair—"

"We'll come up with something," Uncle Daney said. Cole could see why Pop didn't like to tackle him directly. He made one more try.

"What if we don't? What will you do?"

"Send him back to the log camp," Uncle Daney said.

"Hate to, though. Most loggers don't handle a horse the way I do."

Cole thought of Roger Allard's bulging muscles, of the men at the pulling contests, leaning back on the reins with all their weight. He didn't want to send Nip way up north to a logging camp.

"People win prize money at the fair," he said. "The cattle show, baked stuff—" Maybe he could show the steer—if he could train him to lead. Maybe he could bake a cake . . .

"Somethin'll come to us," Uncle Daney said.

Cole went into his stall and closed the door. He wasn't so sure something *would* come, and he didn't want to wait around for it. But he couldn't think of anything else to do.

The first thing that came to them was the cart.

Ray West and a carpenter friend and Cole built a ramp along one side of the barn, so Uncle Daney could get up into the cart. They used some wood that was stored in the back of the barn, some wood Ray had around, a little new wood, so that the ramp was all different shades of weathered pine. That made it look a little ramshackle, but really it was straight and strong and made a long, gradual slant up to the level of the cart.

When the ramp was done, Ray brought the cart over in the big truck he used to carry his horses around. There were two old men with him to help unload it.

It still wasn't an elegant cart. It was square and high off the ground, and it had fat rubber tires, like a truck. It was bright red with a yellow pinstripe. Cole had painted the pinstripe on himself.

"Goodness!" Mom said when she came out to take a look. "What a job you've done, Ray!"

"Had plenty of help," Ray West said. He looked excited. "Hook her up, Daney! Where's Nip?"

Cole ran to get him, and Nip was brushed and harnessed in record time.

"Think you ought to put some reins on him, Daney?" one of the men asked. "Might startle folks, they see you drivin' without 'em."

Uncle Daney cackled. "All right, put some on. Braided twine there on the wall—ought to be long enough."

While the reins were being put on, two more old men in a pickup truck stopped by. Ray West introduced them. Mom made coffee.

Suddenly everything was ready. A man stood at Nip's head, and Cole and Ray West picked up the shafts and pulled the cart into position behind Nip. It rolled smoothly and easily. Ray buckled the straps around the shafts, showing Cole how it was done. Then he led Nip around the yard a few times. Nip turned his ears back, listening to the sound of the cart behind him, but he didn't seem alarmed. He was used to pulling all kinds of things.

"Time to try it out, Daney," Ray West said at last. He

led Nip over to the ramp, and Uncle Daney wheeled himself up it. They had measured right. The platform was exactly the same height as the back of the cart, and Uncle Daney rolled smoothly into it. He wheeled up to the front.

There was a seat there for a passenger and a wide empty space for Uncle Daney's chair. There was a bar that came down behind the chair and locked in place, so the chair couldn't roll backward. Uncle Daney put it down behind him and picked up the baling twine reins. He looked down at all of them. His eyes were as bright as a bird's.

"Lou?" he said. "There's an empty seat up here."

Mom looked pleased—and worried. She climbed up beside Uncle Daney.

"Boys," Uncle Daney said, "I'm takin' this pretty gal for a spin. Nip, walk." Slowly Nip crunched down the driveway. At the road Uncle Daney pressed a switch on the dashboard of the cart. A blinker came on. He turned out onto blacktop, and the bright red cart went down the road, both lights flashing now like the hazard lights on a truck.

"Think that's safe, Ray?" somebody asked. "If they was to get in trouble—"

"Oh, heck, they won't get in trouble! That horse'll do anything Daney asks him to."

Ray West and Cole went into the barn and put down blocks for the cart to rest against when it wasn't being used. Cole kept listening for Nip's hooves in the drive-way. Mom could handle Nip, too, he was thinking. But it might have been better for him, or Ray West, to go out with Uncle Daney the first time.

Half an hour passed. They didn't come back. The cof-fee was cool and gray in the mugs, and everyone stood not talking, watching the road.

Then a pickup came along, going slow, and pulled into the yard in a hesitant way. A man in overalls and a striped cap leaned out the window. "Was that Daney I seen down the road drivin' a red cart?"

"Yes," said Ray West, and Cole asked, "Are they all right?"

"Oh, heck, yes! They'll be here in a few minutes." The man in the cap stopped his truck and got out to wait with the rest of them.

Cole wanted to go down to the road and look, but that would make him feel like a little kid. He scuffed his foot in the gravel and drew tic-tac-toe. Pop's truck pulled into the yard.

"What's going on?"

"Mom and Uncle Daney are out in the cart," Cole said. "They should be back any minute—"

Pop went down to the end of the driveway, and now Cole could go, too. At first they didn't see anything. Then Cole heard a faint crunching sound and a high-pitched cackle, and he saw a small red spot in the distance, coming slowly nearer.

Mom's hair was windblown, and she was laughing. Uncle Daney said, "Whoa," and looked down at Pop. " 'Fraid supper'll be late, Bill. Your wife's been out with me, joyridin'."

Pop looked at the bright new cart and at Mom laughing down at him. He turned and looked back at the little knot of old men in work clothes, waiting by the barn door. Cole thought he looked trapped.

|| CHAPTER EIGHT ||

COLE DIDN'T WANT Pop to be trapped.

They *had* to keep Nip. As soon as they had the cart, there was no other choice. Uncle Daney was out every day, sometimes alone, sometimes with Cole. Often he drove into abandoned fields and sat while Nip grazed. The grass they had seeded was growing well, but it was still too young and tender for hard grazing. Now that he had another set of wheels, Uncle Daney could take Nip farther and graze him more.

He went visiting. He stopped in people's dooryards, and they came out and leaned on the cart to talk with him. He stopped in the middle of dirt roads to talk with men who leaned out the windows of their pickups. It didn't matter that he couldn't get out of the cart alone. Half the people around here visited only from the cabs of their trucks and left the engines running. Uncle Daney was just like everybody else now. Pop couldn't take that new freedom away from him.

On the other hand, there still wasn't any money. Pop had sold a cord of wood to one of Uncle Daney's friends the day the cart came. Cole figured he could claim a little of that money for Nip if he had to. But the chain saw needed repairs, and when Cole saw the bill for that, he understood the hole Pop was in.

He looked in the help wanted ads every night. Nobody seemed to need *his* help.

While he thought, summer was passing too quickly. Cole measured by the work they did. One bushel of beans canned. One log down the Hogback. One tree cut before Nip came back. Day by day, log by log, it went.

In August Uncle Daney taught Cole how to find chanterelles. "Them're the one mushroom *I* dare eat!" he said, and he told enough stories of towering loggers dead in a moment to keep Cole from wanting to experiment. He found plenty of chanterelles, but not enough to sell. Mom fried them up in butter.

Then it was blackberry time, and Uncle Daney drove Cole far afield to overgrown roadside pastures and the edges of new clearings. "You check over there?" he'd ask. "Oh, there's a big, juicy feller! Get him—no, to your left! Higher!" Blackberrying with Uncle Daney was a test of Cole's patience.

They did get enough berries, though, to send into town

with Pop and sell at the store. That was enough to keep Cole going. Five dollars, eight dollars, ten dollars . . .

Once they went farther than usual and came on a place where the Allards were cutting firewood. There was a rough road into the woods, littered with flakes of bark, and Uncle Daney turned in. Logged-off areas were good for blackberries, and they grew thick along the edge of the road, berries the size of Cole's thumb.

Uncle Daney pulled the cart close to one side of the road. That way he could reach from where he sat and pick the highest berries. Not many went into the bucket. Ahead, behind, Cole pushed deep into the bushes. He was so scratched already, so mosquito-bitten that he hardly noticed anymore. All he saw were blackberries: one for hay, one for jam, one for pie, one for mouth. There were chain saws working in the distance. Nip stood patiently, ears pricked toward the sound.

After a while they heard a truck. Uncle Daney pulled Nip farther to the side. Cole went to stand at Nip's head, just in case.

"He won't go nowhere," Uncle Daney said. "He knows trucks."

When the truck finally growled into view, it seemed to fill the narrow road completely. Cole tightened his grip on Nip's bridle, but Nip just watched, mildly interested, while the truck slowed down and crawled along the other edge of the road.

It was a tall stock truck, and there were horses inside.

Cole could hear their hooves thump and scrape on the floor. There was a sign on the truck door: ALLARD BROS. FIREWOOD. The driver waved as he passed, and in the passenger side of the cab Cole saw Roger's surprised face.

"If them fellers are leavin' for the day, must be time for us to go, too," Uncle Daney said. "You keep on pickin', Cole. I'll drive up the road a piece and find a spot to turn around."

The sun was down by the time they hit blacktop again, but there was no real reason to have the flashers on. Uncle Daney just liked the effect on passing drivers, Cole thought.

When they came to Ray West's house, Uncle Daney pulled into the yard.

"Ray's out back with the horses," Mrs. West said, coming to the door. "Just drive around the barn."

"I might just's well talk with the boss," Uncle Daney said. "This horse's feet need trimmin'. Will he do it in trade for some blackberries?"

"He most certainly will! Go around back and tell him."

Ray West had his team hitched to a log. Out in the pasture he had six orange road cones set up in pairs, not very far apart. A green tennis ball was balanced on top of each cone. As Cole and Uncle Daney came around the corner, Ray West drove between one pair of cones, turned sharply, and headed for the next. The end of the log brushed one of the cones; it teetered, and the ball fell off. Ray West turned to pick it up and saw them.

"Well, hello! You runnin' the road again, Daney?"

"I been workin' all day," Uncle Daney said. "What d'you call *this* game?"

Ray looked down at the ball in his hand. "Oh, I'm just practicin' for the fair."

"What do you mean?" Cole asked.

"The Farm Horse Contest. You never heard of it, Cole?"

Cole shook his head.

"Well, it's no wonder!" Ray West said. "They put us on Friday night, the night the fair opens. Figure it's not interesting enough to have on Saturday, when most of the folks actually come!"

"But what is it?"

"Well, it's a bunch of . . . games, really. Log skiddin', pullin' a wagon around an obstacle course. It's based on how a farmer really works with a team. Chance for a feller like me to have a little fun, win a little prize money."

Cole felt himself go still all over.

"So you got to not knock off any of them balls?" Uncle Daney was asking, as if nothing had occurred.

Cole leaned forward and interrupted. "How much prize money?"

Ray West looked surprised. "Well, now, it varies from year to year. Usually fifty dollars for first place, and it goes down by ten dollars for each placing, so second would be forty, and so on."

"And is it just for teams?" Cole asked. "Or can a single horse come?"

"Well, most people *work* a team, so that's what they bring, but there's a Single-Horse Skid— Hey! I never thought. You want to go, Daney? About ten miles. You could drive over yourself Friday morning."

Uncle Daney seemed slow to answer. Cole aimed a swift kick at the near wheel of his chair, jolting him a little.

"Might be fun," Uncle Daney said. "When is it?"

"Week from tomorrow." Ray came closer and looked into the back of the cart. "Oh, hey! Blackberries!"

Before they left Ray West's, Cole had seen the class list for the Farm Horse Contest.

There were two classes Nip could go in: Single-Horse Log Skid and the Egg and Spoon Race. Cole wasn't too sure about Egg and Spoon.

"Can Nip be ridden? Have you been on him?" he asked. They were on their way home now. Nip's feet had been trimmed, and they'd had dessert and a cup of coffee with Ray West and his wife. Now it was dark enough for the flashers to be really useful.

Uncle Daney didn't answer for a moment. He was leaning forward, elbows on his knees, the baling twine reins slack in his hands. "Ay-yup," he said finally. "I been on him."

"Then we can go in Egg and Spoon—if he'll let me ride him. Will he?"

"Oh, yeah."

"If we win two first prizes," Cole said, "that's a hundred dollars! Plus there's a hundred-pound bag of grain for every horse that enters. We'll have to practice all week!"

Uncle Daney didn't answer at all this time. Cole looked at him. He couldn't see well enough to make out Uncle Daney's expression.

"What's the matter? Don't you want to do it?"

Uncle Daney rasped a hand across his bristly chin and sighed. "You're a lot like your grandpa, Coley. Lean into the collar and keep on pullin' till you get what you're after."

Cole didn't know what to say. His grandfather hadn't liked Uncle Daney. Had Uncle Daney liked Grandpa? His voice had sounded—what? Sad? Angry?

The trailer lights came into view. Nip lifted his head and broke into a trot.

Mom and Pop were eating supper at their own table tonight, and Cole went in with them. Suppers together was something Mom had insisted on when he moved out to the barn. Tonight Cole was glad of that.

He told them about the Farm Horse Contest and, after

a moment's wondering if he ought to, about the prize money.

"I guess I'd heard about that," Pop said. "One of the Allard brothers works part-time with us, and they always go."

Cole remembered the big Allard truck driving past them that afternoon and the sound of horses in back. The Allards worked their horses every day of the week. How could they not win?

But who had more years of skidding logs than Uncle Daney? What horse was any better than Nip?

"Well, it's a chance," Pop said. "Have to say I've got a lot more faith in that horse than I did a few months ago. Like to keep him around if we can."

"And how will you get there?" Mom asked, and quickly answered herself. "Of course, you'll just hop in your chariot and go!"

Cole waited. He hadn't felt as if he was asking permission, but it would be just as well to have it.

"Well, it does sound like fun," Mom said. "And there's a band at night, Bill." Before Mom and Pop bought this place, when money was not quite so tight, they used to go dancing once in a while.

"What time does this thing start, Cole?" Pop asked.

"Five sharp."

"I'll see if I can get off work early," Pop said. "If you'll pack us a picnic supper, Lou—"

           *   *   *

That night, as he lay in bed, thinking ahead to the fair, Cole heard music coming from Uncle Daney's stall. At first he thought it was a radio, but the sound kept starting and stopping and picking up again. He got out of bed and went across the aisle.

Uncle Daney was sitting up in bed. It looked strange, as always, to see how thin and flat his legs lay under the blanket when most people would have bent their knees. Uncle Daney had a harmonica, and as Cole watched, he played the first few bars of a slow, sad tune, stopped, and shook his head.

Cole was about to back away and leave him alone. But as he moved, Uncle Daney caught sight of him.

"Wake you up?"

"No." Cole came into the stall. "What's the matter? Don't you remember the rest of it?"

"Used to keep time with m'toe," Uncle Daney said, looking down at the small, still bumps his feet made in the blanket. "Tryin' to figger out how to do it now."

"Maybe try something livelier?" Cole suggested.

Uncle Daney glanced up at him. "Ay-yup, I'm a-wallowin' in self-pity, boy, and I'm enjoyin' it." He stared so hard at his feet that Cole looked, too. He almost expected to see them move. It didn't seem possible that anything so small could resist.

After a minute Uncle Daney looked up. For the first time in a long while Cole noticed the lines in his face, running wearily downward. But Uncle Daney's blue eyes were as alive as ever. "You're right," he said. "How about a dance tune?" He lifted the harmonica to his mouth, and its thin, wailing voice quickened. At first the rhythm was unsteady, but Cole started to thump time with his foot on the floor. Uncle Daney's eyebrows waggled thanks above the harmonica, and he swung into the chorus. Then he put the harmonica down.

"Oh, we had some dances!" he said. "Some of them were pretty bad men, but we had fun. I ever tell you how Big Ed Davies danced a hole in the bunkhouse floor?"

"No," Cole said, settling down at the end of the bed. As he listened, he closed his eyes. He could see the boy in the old picture, dancing.

|| CHAPTER NINE ||

THE NEXT DAY it rained, and they couldn't practice. Then they had to wait a day for the ground to dry out. Then Mom wanted the cucumbers picked, and she wanted help making pickles. Cole and Uncle Daney sat out in the shade beside the barn and sliced cucumbers into a big bowl, Nip grazed in the pasture, and they made no progress.

Uncle Daney didn't seem to mind. He breathed the hot, tangy pickle smell floating out the trailer windows and closed his eyes. "Smells like home," he said. Cole squirmed and cut faster.

Finally all the cucumbers were sliced. Cole ran out to get Nip and harness him. He got some sap buckets from the back stall, and he set them up in a pattern like Ray West's road cones. Then he drove Nip out to the log pile,

with Uncle Daney following more slowly. He wrapped
the chain around a log and hooked the whippletree onto
it. Uncle Daney came up, the wheels of the chair
streaked with mud.

"You'll have to hitch him yourself," Cole said. This was
the part he was worried about. "Can you reach?"

"No way to know without tryin'," Uncle Daney said.
He turned Nip in a neat, small square—neater, and
smaller, than Cole could ever manage. Then he backed
Nip one step. "All right, whoa." Nip's heels were very
close to the whippletree.

Uncle Daney brought the chair up close and un-
snapped the tug from the ring it was hooked to. That
was the easy part. Holding the end of the tug, Uncle
Daney reached down for the whippletree.

Too far, Cole thought. He can't do it. Uncle Daney
could reach as far as his toes, but the chair held him up
so his feet were a few inches above the ground.

Uncle Daney sat up, red in the face. "Nope, can't
reach. If you was to get me somethin' with a crook on
the end: a cane, or a crowbar—"

"Be right back." Cole ran to the barn for the crowbar.

Uncle Daney was still holding the tug when Cole got
back. "That ought to be just about right," he said, taking
the crowbar in his free hand. He leaned over, caught the
crooked end under the whippletree, and lifted it high
enough that he could catch hold and hook the tug into
it.

"Well, that's one side," he said. He wheeled himself around in front of Nip, who stood resting one back foot, half-asleep, and hitched on to the other side.

"They don't start timing till the log starts moving," Cole said. "So it's okay if you're slow."

Uncle Daney was wheeling around Nip again and momentarily out of sight. When he came into view, he was tucking his teeth into his shirt pocket, grinning. "Pretty near a year since I hooked a horse," he said. "All right, you're the boss. What do we do now?"

Cole explained the course to him. It wasn't the real course. That would be laid out the day of the fair, and it would be a surprise to everybody. But Ray West had told him what it was usually like. Some simple sets of two or four cones to pass between. Some sharp angles from one set to the next, so the driver had to judge closely when to start turning. A row of five or six cones to weave in and out of. A lawn chair for the driver to sit down in for thirty seconds, while his horse waited without moving, without the driver holding the reins.

"That part'll be easy enough," Cole said.

"Well, you never know," Uncle Daney said. "He stands good here to home, but bein' at the fair might excite him some. All right, let's try 'er. Walk, Nip."

Nip and the log passed between the first two sap buckets easily, turned, headed for the second. There was a thump, and one of the buckets went rolling away.

"Whoa," Uncle Daney said. "Couldn't see enough—can't keep up with him."

"Take a wider angle next time," Cole said, setting up the sap bucket. Uncle Daney brought Nip back to the start to try again.

This time he did better through the first set of buckets. But he still couldn't keep up, had to crane his neck to see where Nip was going. . . . "Whoa!" Uncle Daney sounded breathless and wheezy. This wasn't going to work.

"All right, haw, Nip. Walk on." Through the second set: "Whoa." Nip stopped obediently, with the log still between the sap buckets, while Uncle Daney wheeled ahead to the next pair. "All right, gee. Walk on."

"It's based on time, too," Cole said after a minute.

"What's the ground like down to the fairgrounds?"

"It's pretty flat," Cole said, "but it's all grass."

Uncle Daney took a red bandanna out of his pocket and wiped the sweat off his face. "Think you'll have to push me, then," he said. "S'pose that'll be all right with the fair people?"

"I guess so. I'll ask Ray."

With Cole pushing, it went easier. They could keep Nip moving right along, never touching a bucket, never wasting any time making a wide angle when a sharp one was needed. But after twice through Uncle Daney was breathing hard, and his undershirt was soaked with sweat.

"You do it, Cole," he said.

"*I* don't need to practice," Cole said. "I won't be doing it."

"He will. You got to repeat things with a horse, so he knows you mean it."

So Cole tried. It was harder than it looked to judge the distance between the sap buckets and to judge how sharply to turn. He had to say the right thing to Nip, say it fast enough, and then correct Nip, straighten him out before he turned too far. They crunched a couple of sap buckets before Cole got the hang of it.

"You want to try again?" he asked. Uncle Daney was looking rested now.

"Nope," Uncle Daney said firmly. "I been skiddin' logs all my life. What I don't know it's too goldarned late to learn. You go again. 'Twon't hurt you to have the practice."

Cole went, twice more, and the second time he had a clean, fast round. But he couldn't help worrying. Of course, Uncle Daney knew all there was to know about skidding logs in the woods. But skidding a log between pairs of road cones at the county fair *was* different. Skidding logs from a wheelchair *was* different. He wished he could convince Uncle Daney to try again, but he knew he wasn't really the boss here.

"Guess we better stop now," Uncle Daney said when Cole completed his second time around the course. "We're tearin' up the grass pretty good."

* * *

The next day was the day before the fair. Uncle Daney refused to practice again, and Cole couldn't really blame him. When he looked at the grass and saw the slick, deep gouges the log had made, he knew they'd done all they could. It wouldn't help to have money for hay if they wrecked the pasture getting it.

They spent the morning washing the harness with old rags and some of Mom's liquid oil soap. When it was done, it didn't look much different, but Cole and Uncle Daney were covered with gray, dirty soap streaks and splashes of water.

After lunch Mom gave Cole a boiled egg and a spoon, and he practiced for the Egg and Spoon Race.

In Egg and Spoon you rode around the skidding course balancing the egg on the spoon. If the egg fell off, you were out. If you made it all the way around, you were judged on time. "Most of 'em don't make it," Ray West had said.

There was no point putting the harness on just for this. Cole called Nip to the gate, put the egg and spoon on top of the fence post, and then climbed to the top bar. Nip gave Cole a thoughtful look and swung his rump away.

"Here, Nip!" Uncle Daney said sharply. "Over now!" His voice was gruffer than usual. Nip promptly moved back toward the gate again. Uncle Daney winked up at

Cole. "Old devil's got a mind of his own sometimes! Hurry up, hop on!"

Cole jumped and landed astride Nip's broad, warm back. Nip seemed to lurch forward without moving his feet. "Whoa!" Uncle Daney said sharply. Cole reached for his egg and spoon.

"Does he *mind* if I ride him?"

"Nope. He just don't take it serious, is all. He'll do what you tell him, but speak a little sharper."

"All right." Cole pointed Nip roward the sap buckets. He put his thumb on the egg this time and held on to Nip's mane with the other hand while they went around the course. He did have to speak more sharply, and he saw Nip's ears going back and forth, instead of settling into the serious angle they stayed at when he was working. But it didn't feel like this was going to be hard. Nip's walk was smooth and slow, and he didn't do anything suddenly. Cole took his thumb off the egg and started around again. He watched it closely. It never rocked in the bowl of the spoon.

Well, this was easy! "Will he trot?" he asked Uncle Daney.

"Ay-yup! Cluck a few times with your tongue." Uncle Daney made a clucking sound himself. Nip pricked his ears toward Uncle Daney, as if surprised, and started to trot.

Cole had ridden a trotting pony before. He remembered bobbing up and down so quickly that his eyesight blurred. This was nothing like that. Nip's trot was slow motion, one big, slow, pillowy jounce and then another. They were headed straight toward a sap bucket. "Whoa," Cole said. Nip stopped abruptly, and the egg rolled off the spoon.

Nip pricked his ears at it thoughtfully. He put his head down, nosed the egg for a moment, and then took it in his mouth. Disbelieving, Cole listened to him eat it. The scritchy sound as Nip crunched the shell sent shivers down his back.

"That's nothin'," Uncle Daney said. "Out in the woods he used to eat half a baloney sandwich every day. With mustard!"

Cole swung one leg over Nip's lowered neck and slid down his side. "Guess I won't trot him," he said. "Sure you don't want to practice again?"

"Ay-yup. Want to shine up my wheels and wash m'face and see if your mother'll give me a haircut. Usually a lot of pretty women at the fair, aren't there?"

Cole gave up. Nip wasn't the only one who wouldn't take some things seriously.

|| CHAPTER TEN ||

EARLY FRIDAY MORNING they set out.

A heavy fog hung low on the Hogback. The sun was shining above it, and the fog's brightness stung Cole's eyes when he led Nip out of the barn. The wheels of the cart rolled smoothly over the gravel as he brought it around to the side of the barn, where Uncle Daney was going up the ramp—so slowly, working so hard. Cole's gut was tied in a hard, nervous knot. He thought if *he* had to go that slowly, he'd burst. But Uncle Daney was grinning, his mouth sunken, false teeth wetly outlined in his shirt pocket.

"Ready to go?" He dropped the safety bar behind him and picked up the reins.

Mom came out of the trailer as they started down the

driveway and handed Cole a paper bag. "Your lunches. Uncle Daney, drive safely!"

"Oh, Lou, don't fuss. We ain't goin' but ten miles." But they were going into town, straight through town, out the other side. There were a lot of things in town that might frighten Nip. Cole looked at the limp twine reins, frayed and fuzzy, no thicker than his finger. They might make a passing motorist feel more comfortable, but Cole knew there was no way those pieces of string could really hold Nip.

Uncle Daney leaned forward and hit the button for the flashers. They drove straight into a bank of fog.

For a long time they could see no more than the road-side trees and bushes. Uncle Daney sang as he drove, in a high, chirpy tenor—old logging songs and cowboy songs. He made Cole help him with the choruses. Cole hated singing in school and usually just moved his lips. But he figured he couldn't spoil Uncle Daney's singing, and Uncle Daney told him he didn't sound half bad. The knot in Cole's stomach loosened for a while.

But as the fog burned off and the sun came out, they came to the crossroad, the farthest they'd ever driven. This meant turning onto a bigger road, with more traffic, tractor-trailers and dump trucks. Cole leaned forward in his seat, ready to grab the reins.

They hadn't been on the main road five minutes when a big yellow dump truck came around the corner toward them. Cole heard himself gasp. Uncle Daney took a hand off the reins and reached over to pat Cole's knee. "Easy there." Nip pointed his ears thoughtfully at the dump truck and walked on without faltering.

"Better calm down, Coley," Uncle Daney said. "We got a long way to go."

Nip was strong, steady, and untiring. But the clock on the church said one-thirty by the time they hit Main Street. Their lunch was long since eaten, and both of them were hungry.

"Took longer'n I thought," Uncle Daney said. "Guess I'll ask Ray to bring him back tonight."

"You don't think he'll be too tired for the contest?"

"Nope. Wearin' his feet down, though, walkin' on this hardtop. Next year we'll put shoes on him."

Next year. Uncle Daney was taking it for granted. But, Cole thought, even if they won both classes in the Farm Horse Contest, that was only half the money they needed. Where was the rest going to come from? He sat running the numbers through his head again, hardly noticing the stares they got—big red horse and big red cart, clopping down Main Street, stopping at the traffic light.

A lot of people waved. Cole thought it was funny that Uncle Daney, stuck in a wheelchair at their out-of-the-way place, should know so many people here in town. Then he noticed that one person waving was Brie Alexander. She was waving at *him*. He felt his face get as red as the cart, and before he figured out that he should wave back, it was too late.

The fairground was on the other edge of town. They turned off the street at the sign and headed downhill, toward the sound of hammering and voices. A man was organizing the ticket booth, and he seemed surprised to see them.

"Fair doesn't start for another three hours," he said.

"We need to rest this horse before the contest," Uncle Daney said.

"Oh, you're competitors." The man stuck a pink card into a crack on the cart's dash. "Go on down then. You'll be at the far end—and keep him down there, so he doesn't leave anything for the city folks to step in."

They drove through the grounds, where people were setting up booths and carnival rides, cooking sausages and popping popcorn. At the end two men in blue T-shirts were roping off a big section for the Farm Horse Contest. They showed Cole and Uncle Daney where to tie Nip, and they lifted Uncle Daney down out of the cart, wheelchair and all.

Cole unhitched. He took Nip's bridle off, and at Uncle Daney's suggestion he lifted the collar and wiped Nip's sweaty shoulders with an old towel. Then he got the hay out of the cart—half of one of the bales Pop had bought for the calf this winter. He put it in front of Nip, and Nip lowered his head to it peacefully.

Uncle Daney yawned and stretched. "Oh, I'm tuckered! Think I'll catch forty winks." He settled his chair in the shadow of the cart and closed his eyes.

Cole sat on the ground beside him, with his back against the cart's tire. Sleep was out of the question, but he could rest and watch the men walking to and fro, laughing. . . .

When he opened his eyes an hour later, Uncle Daney was gone.

Cole looked toward the midway. There were lots of people there, bright spots of color moving against the bright background of tents and signs. He couldn't see a wheelchair anywhere.

Some people were setting up a loudspeaker system in the back of a pickup truck. Cole walked over toward them, and the lady who was testing the system looked up. "Oh, you're awake! Your uncle met somebody he knew. Said to tell you he'd be right back."

Cole went back to the cart and waited. He watched the men in blue T-shirts set up the road cones and the tennis balls. Then they put up signs, showing the pattern to follow through the cones. Cole memorized it. Uncle Daney should be doing this! he thought, but Uncle Daney wasn't back yet.

A big truck pulled in, and a team of black horses was unloaded. The horses were much bigger than Nip, tall and broad and shiny. Cole watched a big man harness them, and then Uncle Daney came back. An old man in overalls was pushing him because Uncle Daney's hands were full—a plate of sausage with peppers and onions and two big cones of cotton candy.

"Mom's bringing supper," Cole said. Uncle Daney shouldn't be going around spending money. They were here to *make* money.

"I never been to a fair where I didn't eat m'self sick," Uncle Daney said, "and I'm too old to reform." He handed the plate of sausage and a cotton candy to Cole. The sausage had been smelling good to Cole for half an hour now. It tasted just as good as it smelled.

After he'd finished eating, Cole showed Uncle Daney the pattern for the Single-Horse Log Skid. Uncle Daney looked at it for a minute and traced it with a sticky, pink-stained finger. Then he turned away to watch the trucks come in and the teams unload. Cole squirmed and read the pattern again. He'd be right behind Uncle Daney, pushing, he reminded himself. He'd be able to whisper in Uncle Daney's ear.

Now there were a dozen teams in the little tie-up area: huge horses, bays and sorrels and grays. They all were in harness, and people were driving them around, each horse separate but looking toward his mate, some of them moving together stride for stride, just as if they were in double harness. Nip stood beside the cart, pointing his ears at them. He looked small and humble.

Ray West arrived, with giant Cloud and Pewter. Shouts rang back and forth, and Uncle Daney and Cole were

introduced to more people than they could possibly remember. The Allard brothers pulled in with two big
trucks, four big teams. Roger was there, working with
all the rest of them.

Now the loudspeaker crackled to life. "Welcome to the
fifth annual Farm Horse Contest here at the Richfield
Fair. We're ready to start the first class, the Single-Horse
Log Skid. Anybody that hasn't registered better come up
here now."

Oops! Cole thought. He went up and put their names
down, Uncle Daney for the Single-Horse Log Skid, himself for the Egg and Spoon Race. While he was doing
that, the first driver started.

There were three logs lined up at the start. A chain
was wrapped around the middle log, and hooked to the
chain, a whippletree. The man drove up to the log,
dropped the reins on the ground, and tried to hitch on.
His horse swung around restlessly. He had to speak to
the horse and bring him back in line with the log. Finally
he was ready, and the horse started walking.

Until this moment the pairs of orange cones had
looked far apart to Cole. But as he saw the huge horse
heading toward them, he realized this was impossible.
No one could do this.

First the horse and then the whole length of the log
passed between the cones. Cole heard a sigh from the
people near him. Nobody else had thought it possible
either.

He went back to Uncle Daney, who was sitting near the cart with an ever-growing crowd of old men. There was a lot of talking and joking, and Cole could hardly get close. He wanted to be next to Uncle Daney, so they could comment together about this driver, plan their strategy. But Uncle Daney didn't seem to be paying as much attention as Cole had hoped.

The next obstacle was four cones set up in a rectangle. The horse went through without touching, and the driver started to turn him. Too soon, Cole thought, and he heard Uncle Daney grunt. So he *was* watching! The log rolled with the turn and knocked over a cone.

Next the driver had to zigzag through five cones set up in a line. His horse turned hard, in big fat loops. "That'll cost him time," somebody said, and Cole began to feel better. He watched as the log knocked over another cone and a dangling chain from the whippletree picked off a tennis ball.

Now the lawn chair. The driver dropped his reins on the ground and sat down, while the timekeeper looked at his watch. The horse stood with his ears back and his head high, and the man watched sharply, as if he didn't believe the horse would stand. At the end of thirty seconds he jumped up and grabbed the reins and walked the horse back to the starting point.

Now he had to line the log up even with the other two logs and perfectly parallel. Cole had spent a long time practicing that, and he wasn't surprised to see this driver leave the log crooked. "We can beat that," Uncle Daney said.

"Nice round for Hank Taylor," the loudspeaker lady said, and Cole heard clapping. He looked to the bleachers and was surprised to see that they were nearly full. Behind the bleachers the Ferris wheel whirled, and the carnival music squawked. The people in the bleachers paid no attention. They leaned forward to watch as the next horse came up to the logs. Cole hadn't imagined that so many people would be watching or that they'd care so much.

The second horse was worse than the first. Now Cole could relax. He put Nip's bridle on, and he untied the baling twine reins from the bit. He got the crowbar from under the seat, ready for Uncle Daney to use when he hitched on. He led Nip closer to the starting line, and he stood beside him, looking around at the big horses, the men in work pants and dark-colored T-shirts—the kind of men you see on road crews or coming out of the factory at the end of a shift. Most of them were older. Only the Allard brothers seemed as young as Pop. They stood a little apart, making a crowd on their own with their wives, their children, and their teams.

Somebody hit his shoulder. "Hey, Cole!" It was Roger. "Saw you last week." Roger was smiling, as if it were easier to say something friendly here at the fair than in school.

"Saw you, too," Cole said. He put his hand on Nip's neck.

"This your uncle's horse? Hey, you forgot to put the reins on."

Cole didn't answer, and Roger stood quiet, watching the third man wipe out three cones on the zigzag. Was Roger worried, too? Cole wondered. After a minute he turned away. "Think I'm next."

When the third man was finished, the loudspeaker lady said, "And now we have a special competitor—for his first drive here, Roger Allard, driving Buster. Roger's a member of the famous Allard family"—a cheer went up from the little crowd of Allards—"and he's the youngest driver here today. Roger's twelve years old. Let's give him a big hand!"

Claps went up from the crowd in the bleachers. Cole saw Mom and Pop over there. Pop had his good blue shirt on—

"How old are you, Coley?"

Cole jumped. Uncle Daney had wheeled over to him, out of the crowd of old men.

"Twelve," Cole said. "I'm twelve, too." He watched Roger drive his bay horse up to the log and try to hook on. He was driving the way the men drove the pulling teams, leaning back on the reins, his arms bulging. Uncle Daney shook his head.

"Seems to me if a feller's got muscles, he uses 'em,

instead of usin' his brain. Now this kid can no more *hold* that horse than a fly could, but he don't know it!" Uncle Daney gave a cackle. "Bet ye the horse does, though!"

Cole watched as Roger hitched. The bay horse wouldn't stand, and after a minute one of the Allards had to come over to hold it. The tips of Roger's ears got red, and Cole felt sorry for him. He didn't know if he wanted Roger to do well or not.

Roger made it through the first set of cones and swung the horse around. He looked small now, to Cole, and he was pulling hard on the reins. The horse went crooked and wiped out two of the next four cones.

Turn again; now the horse was heading straight toward the ropes. When Roger tried to turn him, he just kept going. People sitting near the ropes scrambled up quickly. Roger dug in his heels and pulled hard, and at the last possible moment the bay horse turned. People cheered, and Uncle Daney shook his head.

"He's with them loggin' Allards, ain't he? Ought to know better'n to drive a horse like that." He watched Roger's meandering struggle through the obstacles in silent disapproval.

Cole felt sorry for Roger as long as his back was turned. But when Roger headed toward the finish line and Cole saw the manly, satisfied look on his face, he changed his mind.

"A big hand for a promising young teamster," the loudspeaker lady said as Roger stopped the log, crooked and out of line. Uncle Daney snorted.

"*We'll* show 'em a promisin' young teamster!"

"But I'm not skidding," Cole said. "You are."

Uncle Daney looked up at him and after a long moment put one hand on his stomach. "Think maybe that cotton candy gave me a bellyache," he said.

|| CHAPTER ELEVEN ||

COLE STARED at him. Uncle Daney was the healthiest-looking old man he had ever seen, wheelchair or not.

"But I thought you wanted to!" Cole knew *he* had wanted it: Uncle Daney in his wheelchair out in that ring, showing the teamsters and the old men on the sidelines, the tourists, and Mom and Pop how it was done. He'd been looking forward to that almost as much as to the prize money. "Anyway, you've got a lot better chance!"

Uncle Daney shook his head. "I could get through clean, I betcha, but we're still too danged slow. Watch Ray now. Here's the man you got to beat."

Ray West was driving his big silver horse Cloud through the obstacles. Man and horse walked along easily, relaxed. The reins were long and loose, and Ray turned Cloud lightly, skimming through the zigzag in flat, shallow curves. In the lawn chair he crossed his legs and chatted with the timekeeper. He stopped the log perfectly parallel to the others and perfectly even. He had knocked off only two tennis balls. The crowd set up a loud cheer even before the announcer could call for one.

"Go up and change the names, Cole," Uncle Daney said. "And quit aglowerin'."

Cole had registered last, so he had to stand and watch all the Allards go before him—big men, with bulging muscles and red, outdoor faces. Some drove better than others, but none was as good as Ray West. Cole watched closely, noting every place that was hard for them. But they drove so differently, with their muscles, with their high, broad shoulders, arms spread wide, the reins making tight lines back to their tight fists. It didn't seem as if Cole could learn anything. He and Nip weren't going to do it that way.

Finally the last Allard pulled up at the finish line, and the loudspeaker lady spoke Cole's name. Cole's heart beat so hard he thought it must be fluttering his shirt-front. He glanced once, quickly, at the bleachers, where Mom was sitting frozen and Pop had stood up. Then he said, "Walk, Nip," and went up to the logs. As he turned Nip around to hitch on, he heard the slow, wondering murmur of the crowd.

"That's right, folks," the loudspeaker lady said cheerfully. "He doesn't have any reins. That's how they do it in some of the camps up north, so they tell me, so watch close. You're going to see something special."

Cole's face went hot. Why had Uncle Daney done this to him? "Walk, Nip," he said, and as the log started moving, he looked ahead to the narrow space between the cones. "Haw a little. Walk on."

Nip walked through without touching. The log followed.

"Turn him now!" Uncle Daney would be saying if this were their sap bucket course in the pasture. Cole stepped away from Nip, so he could see what angle to take. "Haw, Nip. Haw a little. Walk on!" This was where he had an advantage. Working without reins, he didn't have to stay close behind Nip, where he couldn't see.

He didn't know what to do with his hands, though. He shoved them in his pockets. "Gee now! Okay, walk."

Nip walked along comfortably, his ears at their usual mild angle. When he turned and saw the bleachers filled with people, he seemed surprised for a moment. Cole tried not to see Mom and Pop, but he couldn't help it. They were standing right at the rope now, looking at him. Pop had a big grin on his face, and Mom was smiling her helpless, Uncle Daney smile. "Haw, Nip," Cole said, and looked away from them.

Now the zigzag. That was the hardest part. Cole couldn't think and speak quickly enough, Nip couldn't respond quickly enough, to move through it the way Ray West had. They made fat, time-wasting curves like everyone else. The one time Cole did manage to flatten out the curve, the log brushed a cone, and the tennis ball fell off.

Out of the zigzag, between two more cones—he misjudged, knocked off another ball. And now the lawn chair. "Whoa, Nip." Nip stopped, steady and solid, as if he would stand there all day, and Cole sat down.

He could feel them all looking, their eyes like hard rain on his face. Even though he tried not to and sat looking at his knees, he could see Uncle Daney, his silvery head and the polished wheels of his chair gleaming in the late-afternoon sun. He could see Roger Allard standing with his mouth open, the rest of the Allards talking around him excitedly.

"This is something to see," one of the timekeepers said to Cole, never taking his eyes from his watch. "My grandfather had a horse like this—all right! Time's up!"

"Walk, Nip," Cole said even before he got out of the chair. Nip walked to the finish line. Cole swung him around and stopped the log, even with the others and almost parallel.

"Let's hear it for this young man!" said the loudspeaker lady as the bleachers burst into applause. The sound was loud enough to mute the carnival music for a moment. Cole unhitched from the log, keeping his head bent. As soon as he was unhitched, he led Nip straight into the group of horses behind the starting line. Only then could he lift his head. Even Nip was small here, and behind the giant bulk of Cloud and Pewter, he was hidden.

Ray West was standing behind his horses, the reins slack in his hands. He made a thumbs-up sign to Cole as Uncle Daney wheeled slowly forward to meet them.

When Cole saw the I-told-you-so look Uncle Daney flashed toward the group of old men, all the tightness eased out of his chest. Uncle Daney grinned and gripped Cole's hand. His own hand was still sticky with cotton candy. He held his other palm out for Nip to lick. Cole rubbed Nip's neck, and for a second the three of them were joined in a circle.

Then Pop was thumping him on the shoulders. "Nice job, Cole!"

And Mom was asking, "But your stomach's all better *now*, Uncle Daney?"

Uncle Daney's friends were gathering, congratulating Cole and congratulating Uncle Daney even more. Cole leaned against Nip's warm shoulder. There was so much talk going on he didn't have to say anything at all. He felt more relaxed and happy than he had in a long time. For just a moment he knew exactly who he was and what he looked like, where he fitted in the world. He could measure himself and Nip directly. Nip was a small work horse, and he was the smallest driver—a lot smaller even than Roger Allard. He could see what he must have looked like as he went around the course: a skinny little kid with big work boots on, his hands stuffed in his pockets.

He could even see what he'd be like when he grew up—not big and broad like Roger, like Sherm Allard and like Pop, but little and wispy. Like Mom. Like Uncle Daney. He would always need to do things Uncle Daney's way. He was never going to outgrow that. . . .

"All right, in just a minute we'll be ready to start the team events, but first here's the results for the Single-Horse Log Skid."

Cole straightened, waiting.

"First place goes to Ray West, with ninety points, time of five minutes forty-nine seconds. Second, Cole Tatro, eighty-five points, time of five minutes forty seconds. Third, Sherm Allard, eighty-five points, time five minutes fifty-five seconds—"

"You beat him on time!" Ray West said. "Heck, you beat *me* on *time*! If you'd gotten that log a hair straighter at the end, young feller, you'd have beat me altogether!"

Cole felt complicated now—proud and pleased—but he hadn't won. That was forty dollars, not fifty. He listened to the loudspeaker. Fourth place, fifth place, sixth place . . .

Across the ring, between the huge teams, Cole saw Roger waiting, too. He was pretending not to listen, joshing with his uncles as they coupled two giant horses together to make a team. But when sixth place went by, and Roger's name hadn't been mentioned, he didn't laugh off defeat the way his uncles had. A bright color burned in his cheeks, and his eyes never moved in Cole's direction. There seemed to be an invisible wall in the air that turned Roger's gaze away.

‖ CHAPTER TWELVE ‖

RAY WEST hadn't entered the Wood Load Race. He needed a partner for that. But after Cole had hung the shining red ribbon on Nip's collar and accepted more congratulations—too much, too visible in front of Roger Allard—Ray said he would enter if Pop would help him, and Pop said yes.

"Like to do my share for Nip's hay fund," he said. "Figure I owe Nip about thirty dollars in wood money, too. I've sold a couple cords I wouldn't have had without him."

Cole could have hugged Pop, but not here, in this crowd of men. He was glad to suddenly feel Mom's arm around his shoulders. She gave him a quick squeeze. "Bill, at least take off your good shirt," she said.

In his clean white T-shirt Pop helped Ray West load

the log sled with a half cord of four-foot logs. They worked quickly and neatly, fat old Ray West as strong and easy-seeming as Pop. When the wood was loaded, they climbed on the sled, drove it around a course marked out on half the ring, then stopped and unloaded again, stacking the wood in a neat pile. Cloud and Pewter stood quiet and patient, waiting for new orders.

"I don't know if we'll win," Pop said, coming back to them. His face was bright, and he was breathing hard. "The Allard boys'll be pretty fast. But their horses won't stand like that team of Ray's."

Pop looked happy, Cole thought. It was like on the playground when they finally ask you to play ball. He watched Roger Allard help his father, Sherm, load the sled. Roger worked fiercely, never smiling. He and his father were fast, and Cole waited for the results, hoping. But—

"Ray West and Bill Tatro win the Wood Load Race."

"Ray West wins Team Skidding."

"Ray West wins Ground Driving. Sherm Allard second."

The Allards didn't seem bothered that Ray won all the time. They laughed and shouted jokes. "They're used to it," Ray said when Cole mentioned it. "And I practice a lot. They're too busy workin' their horses to stop an' train 'em."

They might be used to it, but Roger wasn't. Cole

couldn't blame him for feeling bad and keeping to himself.

Uncle Daney seemed to blame him, though.

"Kinda thought that young feller'd be more friendly," he said, and Cole saw how he kept looking over at Roger whenever the talk around him died down or the crowd of old men parted.

The sun had gone down by now, and the air was cooling fast. People were putting on shirts, and Mom asked Cole, "When do you ride? I want to go get the supper basket, but I don't want to miss you."

"It's starting now," Cole said, "but I'm about last."

Most of the events were over now. The last team event was the Wagon Contest: driving a wagon as long and red as a fire engine through an obstacle course. When Cole first saw the wagon, he knew it was impossible, but the good drivers did it with very little trouble. Ray West wasn't going to win this time. One of the obstacles was made of hay bales, and Pewter had picked up a bale in his teeth.

Now the teams were being uncoupled and some horses unharnessed. Cole envied the way the tall Allard brothers stripped the whole heavy harness off a horse in one smooth motion, as if it weighed nothing at all. Seeing the grateful way the horses shook their bodies when the harnesses were off, he worked his hand under Nip's harness in several places, lifted it to let the cool air under, scratched. Nip grunted and twitched his upper lip, as if scratching an imaginary buddy.

Now there were men on big horses, riding around. In the growing dusk, in their green work clothes or bright sweatshirts with the names of volunteer fire departments on the back, they looked like knights to Cole. They were high, and as the horses moved around, the men's heads and shoulders traced a fine, big motion across the sky. Cole stood beside Nip and watched them.

"Mount up, Cole! What you hangin' back for?" Uncle Daney was frowning at him.

Cole turned and climbed up the harness straps onto Nip's back. Nip craned his head around to look back at Cole.

"Now g'wan over there with the rest of 'em!" Uncle Daney said. The first man was starting out with his egg now. The rest were gathering behind the starting line. Cole took a deep breath and rode over to join them. He stopped a little apart. He knew that strange horses sometimes fight if they get too close together. Without reins he'd have no way of stopping Nip.

A moment later Roger rode up beside him. Cole thought it might be an accident at first. Maybe Roger hadn't noticed who he was stopping next to.

"Whoa." Roger pulled hard on the reins and looked over at Cole. "So why do you bother to put a bridle on at all?" His voice sounded like the beginning of a fight.

Cole shrugged. "Looks, I guess." Roger didn't turn

away. "Maybe a bridle puts him in a working frame of mind," Cole said. "Maybe that's why Uncle Daney does it."

"Your uncle trained this horse, right?" Roger asked. "*You* didn't do it?"

"No," Cole said, and he felt the hard knot in his stomach suddenly loosen. He leaned his forearms on the brass knobs of the hames. "It's not fair really. If *you* had a horse trained that way—" He stopped. He had been going to say, You would have beat me, but he didn't really think that.

He heard Roger take a large breath and let it out with a whoosh. "Yeah," he said. "*How* did he train him? That's what I've been trying to figure out."

"I don't know." Cole was amazed. All this time he'd been working with Nip, and he'd never even wondered how a horse like Nip was produced. He looked at Nip's peaceful red ears. How *did* you teach a horse something? "Ask him!" he said. "I think Uncle Daney'd—"

They were interrupted by a groan from the bleachers. Cole and Roger looked over. The first man was riding out of the ring, laughing. An official was picking up the egg.

"Is this hard?" Cole asked. "I haven't been watching."

"Yeah, it's harder than it sounds like." They watched the next man go.

It was easy to see what the problem was. The horse was used to being steered firmly, with two reins. But a rider holding an egg and spoon had only one hand for the reins. The horse was confused, and he didn't want to go around that stupid course again, anyway. He turned in slow circles, and nothing the rider did could straighten him out. The rider started laughing helplessly as his friends yelled jokes. Finally he laughed so hard the egg fell off, only a few feet from the starting line.

"Hey, it's hard-boiled!" Cole said as one of the time-keepers picked up the egg.

"Next, Roger Allard," said the loudspeaker lady.

Roger groaned and started forward. "I'm gonna do *so* bad!"

He was right. He never lost the egg, but it took him nearly fifteen minutes to go around the course. The bay horse stopped at every set of cones or went wide around them. For about three minutes he turned in a small circle in the middle of the ring. Roger was red-faced and grinning when he crossed the finish line, and one of his uncles shouted, "That egg must be pretty near rotten by now, Rog! How many points you lose for that?" Roger laughed and rode over to Cole.

"I didn't drop it, anyway!"

They watched Ray West, as small as a child on giant Cloud, ride calmly and smoothly around the course. Cole wondered for a minute if Ray might try *not* to win this time, now that he knew what they needed the money for. But Ray West, too, had hay to buy. Besides, he was the best. Cole wasn't surprised to see him do so well, and he wasn't even really sorry. He was just ready to go out there and try his hardest.

And suddenly it was his turn.

"You'll win, I bet," Roger said, and he didn't sound as if he minded. Cole had a warm glow in his chest as he rode up to get his egg.

"Here you go," the timekeeper said, handing up the egg on the spoon. Nip turned his head to look at it. "Keep your thumb on it till you cross the starting line."

Cole settled himself securely and gripped one of the hames. "Walk, Nip."

He crossed the starting line, and the timekeeper said, "Thumbs up!"

Nip moved at a steady amble. Not fast enough, Cole thought. Nip had gone faster pulling the log. "C'mon, Nip! *Walk!*" They passed through one set of cones, two, and now there was a long straight stretch. Did he dare trot? Cole looked at Nip's ears. They were moving, forward and then back, sometimes both together, sometimes one at a time. Nip was thinking about something—

Suddenly, as if an iron bar had dropped in front of him, he stopped. Cole lurched forward, and the egg rolled off the spoon.

Instantly Nip put his head down. Cole heard a groan from the thin crowd in the bleachers and from the crowd of drivers. And he heard Nip's big breath whooshing as he hunted for the egg. Then he heard the sound of eggshells crunching, a disbelieving pause, and a shout of laughter. Above it all rose Uncle Daney's high-pitched cackle.

Cole sat there. He had to wait until Nip finished the egg. He heard somebody yell, "Wouldn't he rather have a little salt and pepper?" and he knew he should turn and laugh, as Roger had, make a joke of his own. But he felt like crying. To everybody else this was a game. He was the only one who took it seriously, and he had just lost.

"You don't have to buy this horse hay!" Pop said when the egg was finished and Cole rode back to them. "You can feed him on egg salad sandwiches!"

Uncle Daney cackled. "Or baloney! He done that on purpose, y'know!"

Cole could make himself smile now, and as he slid down from Nip's back, he saw Roger, across the ring, grin in friendly sympathy. Roger's grin made Cole's own smile fit more easily on his face. Still, he was glad to disappear behind Nip and stop pretending.

It was almost completely dark now. On the other side of the fairground a country band had started to play. Horses thudded up ramps, and Cole went with Ray West to get his grain store certificate and his forty-dollar check. He tried to be happy about it. With the fifty-five dollars from Pop, they had nearly a hundred.

Still, that was only half of what they needed. Where was the other half going to come from? Sit by a road long enough, Uncle Daney had said, and everything you need'll come by. But Cole had never yet seen a hundred dollars come walking down that road.

They all gathered at Ray West's truck. Ray was going to take Nip home, unharness him, and turn him out to pasture. He'd come back Saturday morning for the cart. "I don't care much for a band," Ray said, "and I can see you people do." Mom's foot was tapping, and Uncle Daney's fingers beat time on the arm of his chair. Even Pop's head was turned toward the music.

Cole was thinking he might go home with Nip. He might like to sit alone on his bed and think hard about money.

But the Allards had just finished loading, and now Sherm and Roger came over. Beside his father Roger didn't look so big, but Cole could see how big he would be in a few years. Both Allards had funny looks on their faces, almost as if they were feeling shy.

"Daney, Cole, like to talk to you for a minute," Sherm Allard said.

"Lou and Bill, you g'wan over to the music," Uncle Daney said. "We'll catch up." Mom looked surprised and a little unwilling, but Pop was already starting. Cole turned back to the Allards. He didn't understand why they should look nervous, and it made him nervous, too. He leaned on the back of Uncle Daney's chair.

"Like your way of handling a horse," Sherm said after a minute. "You trained him, Daney?"

"Ay-yup," said Uncle Daney. "Trained horse and boy both!"

"Well, it looks safe," Sherm said, "and it looks a heck of a lot easier than *my* way of doing things. I ain't too old a dog to learn new tricks." He looked hard now at Uncle Daney, as if he was trying to see inside him. Roger stood beside him, stock-still and embarrassed.

"I don't know if I should ask you this, the shape you're in," Sherm Allard said. "But you think you could still train a horse? I'd like to have one that could skid logs like that, and a boy that knew how to handle him."

Oh! thought Cole.

Uncle Daney swirled his teeth in his mouth. Cole heard them click and settle into place.

"What d'you mean, the shape I'm in? Still got the use of my brains, don't I?"

Cole stepped from behind the wheelchair. "I'll help." He saw Sherm Allard's eyes on him, and he knew how small he looked. Well, he couldn't help that. Besides, even Roger was too small to hold a work horse.

"Course, them horses of yours've been used all wrong," Uncle Daney said. " 'Twon't be easy."

"I got one at home I haven't found a mate for," Sherm Allard said. "Haven't used him at all yet." He looked from Cole to Uncle Daney. "If you think you could train him, with two boys to help you, well, it'd be worth something to me. I'm not asking you to do it for nothing."

Uncle Daney said, "Oh, I won't take mon—"

Cole put a hand on Uncle Daney's shoulder and squeezed. Uncle Daney stopped in mid-word, and Cole took a moment to work out what to say. He could understand how Uncle Daney felt, proud and generous and friendly. He felt that way himself, with Sherm and Roger Allard waiting for them to say yes. But this was what they'd been waiting for all spring and summer, by the side of that road and in the woodlot and out there in the juniper patch. He couldn't let the chance go by, and after a minute he knew how to do it.

"You can pay us in hay," he said. "If that would be all right."

JESSIE HAAS and her husband, Michael Daley, live in a very small house they built themselves. Ms. Haas is a graduate of Wellesley College, a life-long Vermonter, and the author of such books as *A Horse like Barney*, *Skipping School*, *The Sixth Sense and Other Stories*, *Beware the Mare*, *Chipmunk!*, and *Mowing*. When not writing, she trains her Morgan horse, Atherton, goes on walks with her three cats, and cooks.